I0538862

Blood in the Wings

The First of Severn

J. L. O'Rourke

Copyright 2015
Published by Millwheel Press Limited
(originally published 2012 as The Flyman)

ISBN 978-0-473-31765-2

Discover other titles by J. L. O'Rourke
Chains of Blood: The Second of Severn
Power Ride: An Avi Livingstone murder mystery

Acknowledgements:

While the majority of the characters in the Severn series are fictional inventions of my imagination and are not based on any real person, my thanks to the two real theatre crew who gave their permission to allow me to exaggerate their personalities and reinvent them into vampires. Those people know who they are – thank you. If anyone else thinks that they recognise themselves in a character – I guarantee that it is purely unintentional. Thanks, too, to my cover models, Skip and Tama.

Cover photo by Bethany Nehoff.

CHAPTER ONE

The rain came down red and Severn was gone.

The police asked me lots of questions, both at the theatre and, later, down at the police station but I couldn't tell them much more than that. No, that's not true. I could have told them heaps more, but I didn't. Anyway, I wasn't sure myself. No, don't tell anyone anything. Just answer their questions, get out of here, find Severn and hope the answers are wrong.

"Tell me again, Miss Lowe, take it slowly." The policeman, a detective inspector I think he said he was, kept tapping his pen against the table. It was driving me crazy. The policewoman sitting by the door smiled. That was driving me crazy too.

"What do you know about this Severn?"

I have to think about the answer. I know things about Severn that nobody knows but I hardly know him at all. And I desperately want to keep on learning.

So, really slowly like the cop wants, I start from the beginning again.

"I met Severn two weeks ago when we packed in." It feels like forever.

"Packed in?" the cop inquires.

"Yeah, that's what I said. Pack-in. It's theatre-speak, Get used to it!" This guy was so dumb.

"All right, Miss Lowe," the cop snapped. "There's no need to get abusive. Let's just get on with it so we can all go home."

"Yeah, well don't butt in then!" Okay, it was well after midnight and I was tired and cranky, but he really was a jerk. "I told you, I met him at pack-in. That's when we set up the show in the theatre." I added the last bit slowly, just in case he was as stupid as he looked in his prissy black jacket and his ugly blue tie,

Then, as he still looked blank, I explained.

"Until pack-in the show is all over the place. The actors will have been rehearsing in one place, the orchestra somewhere else and the dancers somewhere else again. The props and the wardrobe have been made at the main rehearsal rooms over the last few months and the sets have been made in a hired warehouse. At least that's how our company usually works."

The cop was rapidly taking notes.

"On pack-in day the set and all the technical stuff such as

the lights and the sound gear arrives at the theatre and the crew take over; rigging, wiring, hauling things into place. It's organised chaos. I love it."

"Why were you there?"

"Mum's been in the society for years. Even before she went to Australia and met Dad. When they split up she came home and joined up again. I go with her."

"You act?"

"No, I'm the family disappointment. Backstage, that's my job. I'm doing theatre arts at school but only because it's easy, not because I ever want to act!"

He was actually writing this down, he really was a jerk!

"But you were at this show?" he asked, looking up from his paper.

"Yeah, I just told you, I work backstage. My theatre arts teacher also happened to be the choreographer for this year's show and she talked to the stage manager who agreed I could work as floor crew, moving bits of set on and off stage when the scenes change.

This year's production is the biggest show we've done. The director decided to have all the scene changes happening with the curtains up but in a black-out and there're about twenty-one scene changes so they needed a lot of crew. That's how come Severn and his lot were there at all. We didn't have enough people to move all the sets by ourselves, or do the complicated lighting the show needs, so the stage manager rang somebody who rang somebody else who suggested Seth Borman.

"Seth Borman," the cop repeated as he wrote the name on his piece of paper.

"That's what I said."

The cop glared at me.

"It was a good idea," I continued. "Even if it is costing the society an arm and a leg. He runs a professional travelling stage crew. Technical wizards."

"And Severn was one of these?" the cop asked.

"Yeah," I snapped back. "I was just getting to that." I carried on.

"Seth Borman's the leader. The head flyman." I could see the cop's eyebrow start to rise with a question so I jumped in first. "Flymen are the guys who work on a little platform about fifteen metres above the stage, hauling the big backdrop cloths and bits of set in and out. They are immensely strong. Seth Borman has an upper body to die for," I added wistfully.

The cop glared at me again. I continued.

"There are six more of them. The women, Olivia and Meredith, work floor crew like I do. So does Aiden, Meredith's twin brother. The older guy, Finn, is the floor electrician. The guy in charge of lighting is a strange little dude they call the Reverend. He's about five foot nothing tall and wears a huge black floor-length coat that makes him look like a miniature version of Darth Vader. I've never seen him without a can of coke in one hand and a chocolate bar in the other.

Severn operates the sound board.

I didn't notice him for the first four days.

Tasha saw him first. When it comes to men, she always does. She's got some sort of inbuilt radar detector that homes in on good-looking men. Mind you, it must be a sending as well as receiving device because they home in on her just as fast.

Tasha was in the show as a dancer. She clicked around backstage in tap shoes and a scarlet bathing costume covered in ostrich feathers, all up in front and out behind. I hate Tasha, she's such a bitch."

"Tasha? Would that be Natasha Moreland?" The cop looked up at me. I nodded. "You said you hate Natasha?" he inquired, tapping his pen again. "Why is that?"

"No, no," I backtracked fast. "I don't hate her really, I just said that, you know, like you do, I don't mean it. She's my friend, actually. She's just, you know, so pretty and everything, And she knows it. She knew it that night, that's for sure."

It was during interval at the final dress rehearsal. We had gone out into the alleyway at the stage door to get some fresh air. It was even darker outside than it had been backstage. We were standing by the open stage door where there was still a bit of light, watching Aiden and Finn playing hackey. I barely noticed Severn and the Reverend leaning against the fire escape off to one side, sharing a can of coke. Until Tasha nodded her head in their direction.

"They're a weird unit, those two."

"You reckon?" I replied automatically as I stole a glance in their direction. They made an interesting study.

Severn, the taller and probably the elder, stood shyly, shoulders hunched and arms folded protectively across his chest.

He had one leg folded over the other so he kind of resembled a nesting stork. In complete contrast was the Reverend. Younger, smaller but full of confidence. He stood firmly, his head back, his shortish brown pony tail bobbing against the collar of his oversize coat as he punctuated a sentence with much waving of the coke can.

"Nicely put together though," I finally answered.

"Hmmm," Tasha snorted. "More your type."

Tasha always says that when she means she doesn't fancy a guy herself. Mind you, she's often right. She was this time. Tasha is into bodies. Big work-out-at-the-gym-every-night type bodies. She was already torn between Seth Borman and the leading man who was the only other import into the company. He'd been brought in from Auckland especially to play the lead as none of our men came up to scratch. A move that was causing ripples of discontent.

I looked again at Severn's long, slender body packed so nicely into his black jeans and long-sleeved black T-shirt with the show's logo and the word "crew" in red so it won't show up on stage, and agreed. Kind of cute.

"Definitely."

"So let's do it." Tasha was into direct action. She pushed herself away from the wall which had been propping her up, flicked her scarlet ostrich plumes and clicked her way across the alley. I followed bemused.

"Spare any of that coke for a gasping dancer?" She broke into their conversation, whipping the can from the Reverend's hand before he could reply. She took a drink and handed it to me before turning back to them. "I'm Tasha, this is Riley. You can talk to us, we don't bite."

The Reverend tilted his head back and managed to look down at her from below. He gave a maliciously sweet smile. "We do." With a wicked giggle he plucked the can from my hand, drained it, crushed it and tossed it into the nearby rubbish bin. "They call me the Reverend. This is Severn."

"Why?" Tasha sounded confused.

"Because he is."

"Not him. You. Why the Reverend?"

"Because I am."

Beside him Severn sniggered. I looked up at him and he flashed me a smile. Without speaking he reached over and felt in one of the Reverend's voluminous pockets, pulled out another can of coke, broke it open and passed it to me.

"You're floor crew, right?" he finally spoke, his voice a light tenor that matched his laugh.

"Yeah. Why Seven?" If Tasha didn't want to know, I did. "Is it because there's seven of you?"

"No. Not the number seven. With an R, like the English river."

"Oh, right." I felt stupid. I also felt the all-too-embarrassing heat of a blush creeping up my neck and into my face. I gave a quick prayer of thanks that it was dark in the alley. Cover it up. "What are you? Follow spot or something? You're not on the floor, I would have seen you."

"Nah," he shook his head with a slight grin. I was sure he had seen my face go red. "I've passed you lots of times. You're right, I'm not floor crew, I'm sound, but I've been backstage every night with the radio mics." He laughed self-depreciatingly. "I didn't think you'd noticed."

Now I felt guilty, like I'd snubbed him on purpose but I was saved from having to reply by a call from the stage door.

"Act two beginners on stage!"

I took another quick gulp from the can before handing it back as we headed back into the backstage gloom.

CHAPTER TWO

When it came, opening night was great. The air was full of nervous tension you could feel. I surprised myself though. I wasn't as nervous as I thought I'd be. I suppose it was because I wasn't on stage. I was used to Mum and Grant panicking about their make-up and their costumes and whether or not they'd forget their lines. Grant? Oh, sorry, he's my stepfather-to-be. Dad stayed in Australia trying to go professional and failing miserably. Grant's the president of the musical society. He moved in with Mum two years ago. Personally I think Mum would have been better off getting a spaniel. Anyway, I was used to their endless last minute rehearsals over dinner and voice warm-ups in the car on the way to the theatre. I didn't need to bother with any of it.

I could hear Mum's contralto voice warbling her character's solo as she fed the cat. I could tell she was nervous. I showered and changed slowly into my stage blacks, pulling my long blonde hair into a plait then winding it into a bun at the nape of my neck. Mum's song ended in a dramatic crescendo just as I pushed in the last clip.

Grant called out to ask if I was ready to leave and I hastily checked my pockets for the last time. Yeah, I had everything, my idiot sheet listing all the set moves I had to make and my brand new black maglight, a tiny torch with a pencil thin beam. I'd saved for weeks to buy it.

I switched it on and it glowed blue through the gel the stage manager had told me to cover it with after the Reverend had told her he could see it bleeding. I must have looked a bit blank at that because Meredith had to explain that this meant it was showing onto the stage and the Reverend could see it from out the front in his lighting box. The wide black-rimmed glasses that covered most of his delicate, almost girlish face must be very powerful.

It wasn't until much later that I realised Meredith can't have heard what the Reverend told the stage manager as they were communicating through the headsets we call comms, but then I often don't realise things until it's too late.

Yeah, opening night was great. The actors channelled their excitement and nerves into their roles and the show was a thousand times better than it had been at rehearsals. The stage manager was smiling.

I caught up with Tasha at interval. Even dripping with sweat she still looked gorgeous. Right then, for a full ten seconds, I really did hate her. I was sweating myself but I didn't look elegant. Just wet. The set moves were all called by numbers and I had hardly stopped for breath. Every time I got one hulking great piece of set stashed away in the scenery dock, they would be calling the number for something else to be on stand-by ready to be pushed on stage. Fake brick walls, garden benches, banquet tables laden with false food, even a piano although Meredith and Aiden did that. I was dying for a drink

I finished my pre-set for the next act then followed Tasha outside into the alley. Severn and the Reverend were already there, propping up the fire escape, drinking coke. Severn looked up as we approached his face lighting into a smile. He held out the coke.

"Here, you look as if you need this."

I sprinted forwards, passing Olivia and Meredith who were huddled together in the shadows against the wall, grabbed the can gratefully and drank heavily.

"Hey!" Severn laughed in protest. "Leave some for me!"

He leaned forwards to take the can back but I was hyped up with all the excitement and feeling a bit silly. I didn't want to give it up so I spun away from him, holding the can at arm's length. I didn't expect to outreach him but I did expect to keep hold of the can. I play netball and I'm reasonably fast and strong. Plus I wouldn't have been surprised if I outweighed him, he was so slim.

I didn't stand a chance, retaliation was swift. First I'm held fast, a strong arm across my chest. Just one arm and even though I'm struggling, I can't move. A soft laugh and the can is wrested from my hand. I'm spun around, facing the end of the alley. Another laugh and I'm all alone. It was uncanny. One minute I'm being held in this warm, if all too brief, embrace and the next minute he's disappeared altogether. Tasha was right. He's a weird unit.

He smelt great though. Not the fake musky stuff Grant sprays around or the sickly sweet muck that the men's dressing rooms reek of. This was subtle, masculine, edible. From being someone I hadn't noticed a few days ago, Severn was fast becoming someone I couldn't forget.

I looked around. He was not in the alley. The Reverend had

gone too and Tasha looked as bemused as I felt.

"Did I miss something?" She shook her head.

"If you did, so did I. Where did they go?"

"Thataway?" Tasha pointed in both directions at once. We looked at each other in silence. "Don't think about it," she finally advised. "Let's go back inside. It's getting cold out here anyway."

We wandered back through the stage door and I followed Tasha mindlessly towards the dressing room stairs. I passed Beth, the assistant stage manager, preparing for the second act. I tried to sound casual as I asked her if Severn and the Reverend were around.

"Oh, no," Beth replied, adjusting her headset. "They're out front. They're on the comms if you want to speak to them."

"They can't be. They were in the alley two seconds ago. Are you sure?"

Beth took off her headset and held it out to me. "Sure I'm sure. Here, talk to them yourself."

I took the headset and pressed it to my ear. She was right. I heard the Reverend's cultured accent deliver the punchline to an extremely uncouth joke and I recognised Severn's light tenor laugh in response. Without speaking, I handed the headset back and walked away.

The second act seemed to fly by even faster than the first. There weren't quite as many scene changes and I had time to see some of the action on stage. Mum got to do her big dramatic solo and got lots of applause and Tasha pulled an even more dramatic scene backstage when she broke the buckle on her shoe. Anybody walking in off the street at that moment would have thought the whole show was about to be brought to a halt by the loss and I think Tasha was a bit put out when Aiden fixed it with a bit of black gaffer tape. With a flick of her ostrich feathers, she flounced off without even a thank-you.

Almost before it had begun, Beth was tapping me on the shoulder and telling me to "stand by move forty two, strike the street," the last move on my idiot sheet. One last rousing chorus number and it's into the curtain calls. Mum's reception was tumultuous and my heart leapt in pleasure for her. I could see Grant grinning too from his place in the back of the chorus line.

When the curtain came down for the last time there were yelps and shouts of glee from the actors as they broke their lines and began a mass orgy of hugging and kissing. I stood back but I still got pounced on by hyped up chorus members as they bounced back to their dressing rooms. Tasha clicked by, waving her arms in the air dementedly. Mum fussed by, too excited to speak. Grant patted me on the shoulder and told me to wait so we could go on to the party together.

I decided against the alley. It would be full of groupies and friends waiting to flock all over the actors. I was just debating whether to stay where I was or wait in the scenery dock when a strong pair of arms wrapped themselves around me from behind. I spun around within them but I didn't push away. Severn applied a little gentle pressure in a light squeeze.

"See you tomorrow," he said. "Your turn to bring the coke."

I pushed back so I could see his face clearly.

"Aren't you coming to the party?"

"No," he replied seriously. "Not our scene. We prefer it back here in the dark. We'll probably pick up a, ah, takeaway on the way home though. Sorry I can't invite you."

"It's Okay. I've got to go with Mum and Grant anyway. I'm sorry you're not coming."

A light tightening of the embrace, almost a hug, and he was gone, through the stage door, flanked by the diminutive Reverend and the dominating Seth.

"See you tomorrow," I called to his departing back.

CHAPTER THREE

I didn't care at all about science the next day.

The party had been really boring. Hardly any of the backstage workers went and those that did left early. So there I was, still in my stage blacks, sitting in a corner watching all the beautiful people parade around doing all the right beautiful-people things and mouthing all the right beautiful-people sayings.

The only good thing was the endless supply of free wine, of which I managed to get several glasses. Actually, it's not true to say it was good, it was terrible but it didn't seem so bad after the first glass and it made the actors' jokes sound almost funny.

The stage manager wafted my direction once. She had swapped her blacks for a floaty pink creation that made her look like a mobile sherbet and she had obviously made a deep inroad into the free wine. Glass in hand, she wobbled towards me, patted me on the shoulder and told me with all the deep sincerity of the almost drunk, how well I had done. She was the only person I spoke to all evening.

Mum and Grant were in the thick of the beautiful people network, circulating in the groups of old-established society members. Tasha was the centre of attention of a group of young males to whom she doled out her attention in equal enough doses to keep them all begging for more.

She was still the centre of attention the next day. Right through interval and lunchtime, and in every available spare minute, she retold her spectacular opening night success to anyone in earshot. The more times she told the story, the bigger star she became. I got sick of hearing it. So I wasn't really listening when they got onto the subject of men and Tasha started talking about me.

"Riley picks up the weirdoes."

"What?" I jerked my head up out of my lunch to glare at her.

She tossed her hair back haughtily and struck a pose.

"The number and his sidekick. You'd call them normal?" She turned back to the others, struck a different pose and explained. "There are heaps of good looking men in the cast and a couple of hunks in the crew and who does Riley end up with? A couple of psychos that don't even have real names."

"They do so!" I realised as soon as I opened my mouth that I had jumped in too fast but it was too late to take it back.

"Oh yeah?" Tasha was triumphant. "Which one? The number?"

"His name is Severn!"

One of the others sniggered. "Does he come after sex? Five, sex, seven," she chanted, mocking my Australian accent.

"With an R. Like the river. And he's not a psycho." By now I was angry. Tasha always managed to do that to me. Like Josh. When he first arrived at the school last year Tasha had fancied him something wicked and she had gone around telling everyone how great he was. Then, when he asked me to go ice skating instead of her, he suddenly became ugly, stupid, desperate. Now she was trying the same trick again, just because Severn looked at me and not her. Stuff her! Not again. I smiled at the others.

"Tasha is just jealous," I said icily. "She might have seen him first but I got him. He's mine." Okay, so it was a lie, half a hug doesn't count as a deal for possession. For all I know he could hug everything; trees, bunnies, policemen even. At that stage all I wanted to do as get a rise out of Tasha and take her down a bit.

I looked around. I had their attention. I gave them a quick description, stressing all the bits I thought they'd like, and I laid it on real thick. There were choruses of "Wow!" and "Lucky you!" and Tasha looked really hacked off.

Anita, who's a terrible gossip, wanted to know more so for the rest of lunch time the conversation swung my way. I told them all about the crew, particularly Seth Borman, but it was pictures of Severn that kept popping up in my head.

In the quiet of the science lab the pictures came back, along with Tasha's words: "psycho", "weirdo". I tried to blot them out. Okay, there was something about him that was different. My mind did a re-run of his disappearing act in the alley. That was weird. Then, just as fast, it blotted that out with a warm fuzzy of his eyes when he smiled. By the end of the lesson I had convinced myself that anything different than normal was better and anything weird was because they travelled around so much. Yeah, that was it. It must be hard to make new friends every few weeks. I moved to New Zealand three years ago and I was still looked on as an outsider. Anybody'd get pretty weird living out of the back of a van.

My science experiment failed. Spectacularly. My head was

so busy spinning out, I didn't hear old Hummer telling us what to do, then I read the instructions all wrong. Anita, who's always my partner, is hopeless at science anyway and wouldn't notice if I was accidentally building an atomic bomb. I reckon I nearly did. Instead of the chemicals mixing with a gentle fizz and giving off a few harmless bubbles, mine turned bright green, hissed viciously then exploded with a bang that made several people scream and got Hummer's attention real fast.

"Riley Lowe!" he screamed across the room. "What do you think you are doing?"

"Making a mistake, I guess," I answered honestly, shrugging my shoulders in doubt. "Sorry."

Hummer stumbled over a suitable reply and glared at those who dared to laugh.

"Clean it up," was the best he could manage.

I did just that, but I still felt pretty stupid and I couldn't get out of there fast enough.

If I had known what was to come, I think I would have stayed in the science lab for the rest of the day. Tasha didn't take too kindly to losing centre stage at lunch time and grabbed an opportunity in theatre arts to snatch it back with a vengeance.

Like I said before, my theatre arts teacher, Dilly, well, Dilys Davenport actually, was also the choreographer for the show so she was using the whole thing as a "learning experience" for the rest of the class. In practice, this meant that Tasha and I had to stand up in front of everyone and make little speeches on "our specialised tasks in the show".

Tasha let me go first. Not to be nice, don't think that. More so that she could top my act and have the final word. Not that topping my act was hard. I hate public speaking. That's one of the reasons I'd rather be crew than be an actor. She's welcome to it.

I mumbled a few words about cues and how "stand-bys" and "goes" are called over the comms from the stage manager to the assistant stage managers, or ASMs as we call them, who relay them to the floor crew, and I answered a couple of almost intelligent questions from the class nerd who had been at the opening night because his mother played second violin in the orchestra. One of the other boys asked a question about spotlights that I didn't know the answer to, so I made up something that sounded intelligent then sat down quickly.

Tasha took the floor. She certainly knew how to get their

attention. The jersey came off as she got to her feet. In another twenty seconds the blouse had been pulled from the waistband of her skirt and knotted higher up, under her upthrust superbra. A flick of a button and all the boys were riveted.

Before Dilly could object, Tasha launched into a spirited rendition of the big production number. The boys were wolf whistling and chanting for more.

I watched Dilly. I could tell she knew Tasha was showing off and she knew she should stop her. But when it came to discipline, Dilly wasn't the greatest. She watched Tasha but she didn't have the guts to do anything. As Tasha came to the end of her little display, Dilly put out a hand and began to rise out of her chair but Tasha still had the upper hand.

"I'm just so wrapped in the dances," she gushed, leaning forwards and showing the boys everything she had. "They're just so fabulous. Ms Davenport's the choreographer. I just think she's so clever. I've always wanted to be a dancer, but since I've been involved in the show, watching Ms Davenport at all the rehearsals, watching how she gets the dancers together and works out all the steps, I've decided I want to be a choreographer. It's my dream now."

Dilly beamed.

I thought I was going to be sick.

CHAPTER FOUR

"So what was all that garbage about?"

I caught Tasha in the hallway after class and spun her round to face me.

"What garbage?" she smiled, all fake and sweet.

"That 'ooh, you're so wonderful, Ms Davenport' garbage, as if you didn't know."

"Oh, you think that was garbage, do you? I thought the only garbage was your pathetic little effort. Moving bits of scenery, ooh, ooh, how exciting!" She was all sarcastic. "You're boring, Riley, very, very boring. It proves what I said before, if the number's interested in you he must be a psycho, or desperate!"

That did it. I was so angry I called her a bitch and shoved her as hard as I could, back against the wall. She gave a sort of anguished grunt as she slammed into the edge of a display case. She straightened herself up, flicking her hair the same way she does before she goes on stage, or goes to hunt down a male. We stood, holding our ground like cowboys in a cheap western gunfight. I was sure she was gong to hit me. I clenched my fists ready to hit back. Then, with another flick of her locks, she chickened out, called me a cow and ran off. I laughed at her departing back.

Well, I laughed until she was around the corner, then I leaned against the display case and shook. I don't normally get physical, not even with Tasha who comes on with this sort of put-down stuff all the time. I picked up my bag from where I'd dropped it on the floor and walked towards the door and home, thinking hard, trying to work out what I was feeling. Half of me was hoping I hadn't hurt her and the other half hoped I had.

Things weren't a lot better at home. There was a letter in the post from Dad, raving enthusiastically about his new partner and baby and asking me to go back to Australia to live with them when I left school at the end of the year. Mum was throwing a major hissy fit in the kitchen, hacking bits off a poor defenceless dead chicken and throwing them into a casserole dish with a viciousness that suggested she was imagining she was doing it to Dad. I ducked for cover, made for my room, which is way at the back of the house, threw a cd on the stereo and turned it up very, very loud.

Dinner was a frosty affair. Mum stressed, Grant dithered and I kept my head down. Grant's into this caring, sharing New Age stuff and kept asking me how I felt about my father, how I felt about my new half-sister, how I felt about Australia. How did I feel? To be honest, I didn't care. A holiday back in Oz would be okay, especially if it's free, but babies? They grab me about as much as cold meat pies. And let's face it, I figured I was up with Dad's real game. He wanted a live-in babysitter. No way! The last thing I wanted was to be even more of an outsider than I was already – a constant reminder to his new family that he had an old one. Give it up, Grant! How do I feel? Irritated! Anyway, I had other things to think about. I had to deal with Tasha at the show and I was beginning to think I should apologise. Again, I was split in two, half of me saying I should and the other half saying I was right and it was her turn to grovel first. After all, she insulted me. And Severn.

As it was, neither event happened. Tasha strutted past in her scarlet feathers while I was doing my pre-set. All I could think of was the mutilated chicken before Mum had hacked it to pieces. I giggled. She didn't speak.

Severn wandered past carrying a handful of radio mics. He didn't speak either but he did flash me a sort of a smile. He looked terrible. If I hadn't known he didn't go to the opening night party, I would have thought he was still hung over. Whatever Seth's crew got up to must have been awesome.

He still didn't speak when he came back past ten minutes later. He just wandered slowly past like he was walking in his sleep, head down and his arms folded across his body in the same wrapped up pose he used when he stood still. I watched him walk past. Finn watched me watching Severn. He stopped me just as I was going to follow Severn and ask him if he was all right.

"Leave him," Finn advised, his strange leathery claw-like hand on my shoulder.

"Is he Okay?" I asked. "He looks sick."

"No, he's just feeling sorry for himself. Severn can be his own worst enemy at times. If you want some advice, young lady, look somewhere else for someone to play with. Severn's not your type."

"My type? How would you know what my type is?"

"I don't" Finn replied with a gruff laugh. "But, whatever that is, he's not it. Just a word of friendly warning from someone who knows Severn better than you do. Stay away. There are things in his head, and his past, you don't want to know about. Look somewhere else, lass, don't make grief, for either of you."

Finn walked off, coiling a cable that snaked off into the wings, and I stood there feeling like I had just missed something important. I wanted to talk to Severn, to see for myself if he was all right, but it didn't happen before the show. I still had heaps of pre-set to do and by the time I had finished sweeping the stage and setting out the park bench for the second scene, Severn was already at his sound board in the front of house and the audience were taking their seats. Oh, well, I'd just have to catch him in the alley at interval. After all, I had remembered to bring the coke.

The show wasn't as good as the opening night. Everyone was tired and, in spite of the stage manager's ra-ra pep talk to the company, both the cast and the crew made mistakes. Even Seth managed to bring in a move too early and hit a chorus member on the head with the weighted end of a flown cloth.

Severn was making hard work of it on the sound board. He was late with his first sound effect and the second one simply didn't happen at all. Half the wings heard the stage manager swearing at him down the comms. I couldn't hear Severn's reply, but I saw Beth wince and I heard the SM's terse "I'll see you later". Severn was in deep trouble.

He certainly didn't look too happy during the interval. He and the Reverend were way down the end of the alley, keeping as low a profile as possible to avoid the SM. I held out the coke.

"Bad hair day, huh?" I broke the silence.

Severn took the coke silently, leaving the reply up to the Reverend.

"Typical second night. Energy's a bit low. It'll pick up. Always does."

"Huh!" Severn didn't sound convinced.

I must have look a bit taken aback at Severn's attitude because the Reverend smiled and nodded Severn's direction.

"Ignore him, his energy level is a bit down tonight too."

"So I gather," I smiled back, throwing one Severn's way as well. "You guys look like you had a hard night last night."

"Do we?" The Reverend laughed. "I didn't think we looked any worse than usual."

"You looked really tired when you walked past me before," I said to Severn.

"Yeah, I am a bit," he finally spoke. "Sorry I didn't speak. You're right, it was a hard night, and a bad day. Thanks for the coke." he handed it back, half empty.

"Oh, there you are," Tasha's voice pierced the darkness of the alley and she tapped towards us. "I've been searching for you everywhere."

Severn groaned.

"Well you found us," I replied with a snap. "What do you want?"

"I want him," she simpered up to Severn, pushed me out of the way to reach him, and stroked his arm seductively. "Come with me."

Severn raised one eyebrow and gave a look of irritation over the top of his tiny tortoiseshell-rimmed glasses. "Why?"

"Because I need you. Just come with me and you'll find out."

"Shout if you need any help," the Reverend called after him as he was led away, looking confused. "What's that all about?"

"Pass," I replied.

"One way to find out. Come on."

The Reverend grabbed my hand and dragged me after him through the stage door. Tasha was leading Severn to her dressing room.

"Interesting!" the Reverend gave an evil grin and glanced at his watch. "I hope she doesn't expect too much from him, she's only got three minutes before they call act two."

"That's disgusting!" I admonished, not too seriously.

"Thank you, I try."

We reached the edge of the dressing room door and peeked around. Severn stood in the middle of the floor, arms folded. Tasha stood facing him, very close, running her hand down his hip.

"I know you keep it in there someplace," she whispered huskily. Beside me the Reverend stifled a laugh.

Tasha felt around Severn's hips seductively while he stood, unmoving and stony faced. She moved until her hand had slipped deep into the pocket of his jeans and then withdrew, clutching his Swiss Army knife. With all the melodrama of a B-grade 1930s screen goddess, she slowly opened the screwdriver blade then sat down, crossed her legs daintily and stroked her hands down them seductively until she reached a purposefully pointed foot from which she removed a scarlet red tap shoe. We watched, fascinated, as Tasha the actress transformed from sex siren to cute little girl as she held out the shoe.

"Can you fix it for me, please," she lisped, eyelashes batting like dying moths.

Severn stood, unspeaking, for several seconds then gave her a look over the top of his glasses that would have frozen hell.

"Why me? I'm a sound operator, not a mechanist." he replied frostily.

Instantly, Tasha was on her feet, stroking his biceps again.

"Please," she purred, "Just one little screw."

The Reverend gave up at that point and dragged me away before he burst out laughing so I didn't see the rest of the drama but I presume Severn gave in and gave out as she was gushing all over him as she delivered him back to us and clicked off happily towards the stage after implanting a kiss on his cheek.

I heard the Reverend's wicked laugh and a muffled comment about a screw as the two men walked away and I saw Severn blush red.

Damn Tasha!

CHAPTER FIVE

In the second act it was my turn to make mistakes. I nearly missed a couple of moves and had Beth poking me in the ribs and hissing frantically, then I made a completely wrong move and stuck a candelabrum in the middle of an outdoor scene. Afterwards the stage manager asked me what went wrong, but I couldn't tell her. All I wanted to do was go home, crawl into bed and pretend the day hadn't happened at all.

Fortunately Mum and Grant were tired too, so they didn't take too long getting their make-up and costumes off. Even so, as we walked down the alley I could see Tasha had been even faster. She had changed into jeans and a top that was so tight she must have sprayed it on out of a can, and she was making sure she gave Severn every opportunity to look straight down the front of it. I walked past, pretending I hadn't seen them, although out the corner of my eye I could tell by the extra wiggle of her hips that Tasha had seen me.

After the grand opening night and party, a botched up second night and a quick cup of drinking chocolate just didn't make the grade and I was glad to hit the pillow. I lay awake for a while, trying to figure out Tasha's game. Then I gave up. Before I went to sleep, I made a decision. At tomorrow's performances I wouldn't think about Tasha or Severn, I'd just do my job and not make any mistakes. They could have each other. So what if he had the most fabulous eyes. Who cared?

I listened to the neighbour's dog barking briefly at something, before I fell asleep.

I slept heavily and woke late. The whole house did. It was after eleven when I finally wandered out to the kitchen. Mum was in her dressing gown, making coffee and it was obvious she had only just woken up too. Still, as long as we got to the theatre by one o'clock for the two o'clock matinee, there was no problem. I've always liked Saturdays.

Grant breezed in waving the morning paper. The review! He laid the paper out on the table and rifled through it hurriedly, looking for the grand judgement, the words that would make or break the rest of the season, not to mention a few theatrical reputations. Down the bottom of page five. Grant read it out loud in his best impersonation of a television news reader. It was good.

Heaps of praise were poured on the leading man, Jason Broderick. Grant was rapt. He had been at the head of the faction on the committee who had pushed to import Broderick instead of using any of our local men and the review had proved him right. He was sure to get re-elected as president now.

Mum was pretty rapt too. The reviewer had singled her out for special mention. "As this reviewer has come to expect, Susan Lowe's rich contralto and superb acting created a character that leapt from the stage into our hearts. Her final solo brought tears to the eyes of many of those seated around me." Heady stuff!

I liked the last bit of the review. The reviewer was impressed with all the technical wizardry and even praised the crew for our "lightening fast but unobtrusive" scene changes. The day was certainly starting off better than yesterday and the party was going to be at our place.

We had a leisurely brunch together, everyone sitting around half dressed, discussing all the things that went wrong the night before. I told Mum and Grant about all the botched up scene changes and about how the stage manager had sworn at Severn over the comms when he missed the sound effect. Grant laughed. He had been on stage at the time and had noticed it not happen, but he doubted if any of the audience would have, as they wouldn't have known it was supposed to.

"Interesting name. Which one is Seven?" Mum asked.

What is it about mothers? Can they all read minds or is mine some kind of witch? I only mentioned Severn in passing but she homed in on the comment like a mosquito to bare flesh. I tried to sound casual but by the look she threw Grant, I don't think I fooled her at all.

"The sound trog," I said quickly. "Does your radio mic."

"Oh," said Mum, acting vague, "The quiet one with the number two hair cut. He's one of the imports, isn't he?"

"Now they're an odd lot," Grant broke in. "I'll be the first to say they seem to be good at what they do, and I know we needed their help to get this show on the boards, but I don't know how to take them at all. They don't mix much."

"I noticed they didn't come to the opening night function," Mum agreed. "Not even Seth Borman. You'd have thought he would have come, at least, just to be polite."

"They're polite enough," Grant continued. "They always speak if you speak to them, they just don't speak first. They're a bit of a closed shop."

"Does it mean something special, his nickname?" Mum asked, reverting to the original topic.

"It's not a nickname." I replied.

"Of course it is! Nobody would call a child Seven."

I couldn't be bothered explaining again that it was spelt differently, so I reached over the table and picked up the programme Grant had discarded there two nights before. I flicked quickly past all the glossy photos till I came to the page listing the technical credits and rapidly scanned the list. Lighting: David Rochester. So the Reverend did have a real name. It suited him. Sound. Where was it? Ah! Sound operator: Severn Jura. I showed Mum.

"Oh, like the street." You could see enlightenment dawn. "It's quite pretty, really," she added after a while. "I wonder if he's foreign."

"City boy, by his accent," Grant put in. "Wellington, maybe."

"That's not foreign!" I protested.

"Aargh, it is to us Southlanderrrrs," Grant retorted in a hideously slurred Southland drawl.

"You're from Canterbury," Mum pointed out, laughing.

"Foiled again! Good acting, though, don't you think?"

Mum gave her critical review in the form of a tea towel, deftly thrown at his head. She checked her watch, "Time to get a move on," rose from the table and began to clear away the dishes.

"I thought I saw Tasha with your sound man when we left last night," she said casually as we hurried the dishes through the sink.

"He's not 'my sound man'," I replied defensively, scrubbing just a bit too hard at a coffee mug. "Yeah, she does seem to have decided to stake a claim. I don't think she actually wants him, she just doesn't want me to get a look in. She does this all the time."

"Does it bother you?"

I hate it when Mum asks personal questions.

"No," I lied. "If he's stupid enough to fall for her dumb little act, they deserve each other."

"Good way to look at it," Mum agreed.

It probably was, if you could.

CHAPTER SIX

I kept the promise I had made to myself and ignored Severn and Tasha. At least, I tried to. I was sweeping the stage when Severn went past the first time, so it was fairly easy to keep my head down and pretend I didn't see him.

After the second time, ignoring him became easier. I walked into the scenery dock to put away the broom and he was hunched over the props table, using their space to lay out the radio mics. I decided to be civil.

"Hi," I began.

There was no answer.

I tried again. "Hi."

Still no reply.

"Stuff you then," I muttered in disgust and began to walk away. That got a response.

"Sorry," he looked up. "I'm a bit busy." His head went down again.

Well, that certainly showed how interesting he found my company! I left him to it and went out into the sunshine. A few of the actors were sneaking last minute cigarettes in the alley. I chatted to a couple of them for a while then wandered back inside. Severn had gone.

At interval the Reverend was propping up the fire escape by himself. He bounced forwards happily as I approached, thrusting a king-sized block of Black Forest chocolate my direction. I broke off a chunk and handed it back with thanks.

"Been jilted?" I asked around a mouthful of chocolate and cherries.

The Reverend tilted his head to one side and looked vague for a few seconds before grinning widely with recognition.

"Oh, Severn! Yes, I suppose you could put it that way. He's not getting a break. He's having problems with one of the shotgun mics, so he's down in the orchestra pit trying to reset it. I don't think I'd want to be the musician who knocked the thing sideways. Severn is not a happy camper."

"He's certainly not a very chatty one."

"Ah, no. Probably not, given the mood he is in today. Don't worry, it's not your problem, Here, have some more chocolate."

"Why?" I asked around a mouthful.

"Why? You need an excuse to eat chocolate?"

"No! Not why the chocolate, why is Severn moody? "What's up with him?"

"Let's just call it a domestic problem." The Reverend made himself comfortable against the fire escape and began to explain. "I don't want to say too much, so I'll just tell you that it's between Severn and Seth. Because of the way we are, we're living on top of each other all the time and sometimes that causes problems. Seth is responsible for Severn being here at all, so it's Seth Severn blames when he gets fed up and wants out."

"So why doesn't he just leave?"

The Reverend paused a long time before answering.

"He can't," he said finally.

"Why not?" It seemed like a pretty stupid answer to me.

The Reverend sighed. "You don't want to know. Just don't ask, okay?"

If the first answer was stupid, this was a complete cop-out. Still, even if I didn't know much about them, I do know when I'm being told to butt out. So I did, walking into the scenery dock and into a battleground.

I didn't realise it was an argument at first. It looked too one-sided for that. Severn was standing, head bowed, shoulders hunched, hands stuffed deeply into his pockets, doing a very good impersonation of a kicked puppy. In front of him, hands on hips and in full flight was the stage manager, and forming the apex to the triangle was the musical director, arms folded, looking every inch the school teacher she was when she wasn't being a musical director. I moved quietly to one side and made myself invisible behind a piece of fake fencing. I wanted to hear this.

Coming in to it in the middle made it a bit hard to catch what it was all about, but I gathered it had to do with the shotgun mic that had been pushed sideways by a musician. Shotgun mics are long, skinny, sensitive things that are placed at the front of the stage and up in the flys to pick up sound from the stage, so it's pretty crucial that they are in the right place. I could understand why Severn was annoyed with a musician who moved one just because he wanted a bit of extra elbow room to play his violin. The stage manager understood this too. What she wasn't pleased with, though, was the threat of violence Severn had made against the offending musician, which the guy had taken seriously, especially considering the cold, determined way Severn had delivered it.

The M.D. kept butting in, reminding Severn that he wasn't a local and generally insinuating that the imported crew had the manners of a pack of water rats. Severn didn't react until she started on the "young boys should respect their elders" bit.

At that, a slow grin began to creep across his face. His posture straightened. He pulled his right hand from out of his pocket, rubbed his unshaven chin, tilted his head towards the M.D. and raised one eyebrow in an expression that managed to include contempt, disbelief and boredom in almost equal parts.

"Really?" he drawled. "Maybe they would, if they were."

Tilting his head the other way, he managed with a raised eyebrow to totally wipe off the M.D.. He addressed the S.M.. "Can I go back to my job now?"

The S.M. nodded.

"Good," Severn snapped. Without another word, he turned and walked away. Inwardly I cheered.

The musical director was still complaining bitterly to the S.M. when I squeezed apologetically between them a few minutes later, carrying the dreaded candelabrum I had made the awful mistake with the day before. The S.M. winked.

"Ball scene," she said without malice.

"Nah," I risked a joke. "Thought I'd try it in the Chinese Restaurant this time."

"Why not?" the S.M. shrugged light-heartedly. "See if Seth can hit it with the street cloth."

As I staggered away under its weight, I heard the M.D. start on the S.M. again. She was one hissed off lady.

"You shouldn't encourage sloppy behaviour...." I didn't wait to hear the S.M.'s reply.

The M.D. was still throwing a hissy fit at the end of the performance. Severn was nowhere to be seen, which was just as well because I don't think he needed to hear the things she was calling him to the violinist as they left the theatre.

"What's his problem?" I heard the violinist whinge dramatically. "It's only a microphone. Anyone would think it was gold plated the way he carried on. Who does he think he is, anyway?"

"A lot more experienced at his job than that idiot is at his, for starters," muttered a voice close to my ear.

"Oh, come on!" I snapped back. "I know you guys are

professionals and you all think us amateurs are pretty second rate, but that guy's been playing a violin for at least three times longer than Severn and you have been alive!"

The Reverend gave a high-pitched giggle. "Hmmm, started on a medieval lute, did he?"

I screwed up my nose at this stupid reply. "Yeah, like if medieval was anything more than 20 years ago, I guess he must have. You're what? Eighteen? He's old enough to be my grandfather. He's old enough to be the stage manager's grandfather. You talk such shit sometimes!"

He giggled again then changed the subject to food. Or, more importantly, pizza, which Severn was off dialling out for. Would I like to join them? Would I what? Give me two minutes to find Mum and tell her I wouldn't be joining them and then it's down stairs to the Green Room. Absolutely. But no mushrooms! I should have added no jalapeno peppers either.

CHAPTER SEVEN

The other thing I should have ordered was no dancers! I don't know which was hotter - the peppers or Tasha.

She hadn't even been invited.

We were all sitting in the Green Room. By all, I mean all the imported crew and myself. Aiden and Meredith, the twins, were sitting at opposite ends of the tatty old couch looking like a set of bookends. Seth was propped between them, arms outstretched over the back of the couch with a hand resting on the shoulder of each twin. It looked like a comfortable and familiar gesture. Olivia was curled up in a huge armchair in the corner, nursing a cup of hot coffee. She had changed from her stage blacks into a one of those flimsy, gypsy style dresses they sell in shops that smell of incense. It was the deepest shade of purple velvet with a front panel of lighter purple lace. Curled up in the chair, with her long, dark hair falling loose, she looked like she could have just stepped out of a medieval castle. Finn sat stiffly to her right on a discarded dining chair. The smallest of them all, the Reverend took up the most space, reclining over a whole couch all by himself.

I sat on the floor.

Tasha came in by accident. We all heard her bouncing down the stairs calling out for Jason Broderick as she approached. So the reply was a concerted "No!" before she had got out the question of "was he in here?" It was just my bad luck that Severn arrived right at that moment, carrying a stack of five large pizza boxes.

"Ooh! Pizza," she gushed. "They smell sooo divine and I'm sooo hungry."

"So stay and join us," Seth beamed from the couch.

"If that's all right with Severn," she batted her eyelashes in his direction. "After all, they're his pizzas."

Severn's shoulders lifted in a non-committal shrug. "Whatever."

Right at that moment I felt like doing several things including telling her she could have mine and walking out, or telling her she could have mine, shoving it, anchovies and all, down her cleavage and walking out, or just being sick. I decided to stay and eat pizza.

"Actually," the Reverend interjected, raising himself off the couch and rescuing the pizzas from Severn's grip, "they're our pizzas and I don't intend to let mine get any colder."

He placed the boxes on the middle of the floor and started prising off their lids. The smell wafted out and I gave up caring about Tasha and her eyelashes, even when she placed herself as close as possible to Severn, who had joined the Reverend on the couch.

In a way it was a pity I didn't have a video camera, she does her best acting off stage. Over the next hour and a half she went through every cute move in the book - including a few suggestive moves with mozzarella cheese that I wouldn't have believed if I hadn't seen them.

Severn's reaction was unreadable. At one stage, while she was spiralling mozzarella around her fingers, he looked at me with a strange little grin but, apart from that, he treated us both as if we were wallpaper. In fact, he didn't speak at all until Seth mentioned the musicians.

The comment was actually a joke about something Seth had seen from up in the fly tower, but just the mention of the word was enough to tip Severn into anger. He stood up, grabbed two pieces of pizza, swore just once and stormed out of the room. Tasha looked dazed.

"Shotguns?" inquired Finn casually.

"Right first time," the Reverend smiled back.

"Oh dear," Finn replied, returning to his meal.

"I think I'll go and see if he needs a hand," the Reverend volunteered. "Say, Riley, do you want to come with me, I'll show you how to work a followspot. It's quite simple and more fun than hauling set around."

"Ok." I agreed. The pizza was nearly finished so it seemed like good timing. It just wasn't so good for the music director.

She had arrived back just as Severn was resetting the shotgun mic again. Unfortunately, a meal hadn't improved her temper either. Finding herself alone with the sound operator, she decided to give him another lecture on how he was expected to behave towards her musicians. Severn retaliated by telling her exactly what he thought of her musicians, their level of education and their possible parentage. By the time the Reverend and I arrived on the stage, they were inches apart, screaming at each other. We stepped in.

At least, the Reverend did. I stood by and watched. He

walked to the centre of the stage and took the M.D. by the arm, directed her into the wings by gentle but determined pressure, thrust her towards me then turned back to Severn who was shaking with rage. I didn't hear what the Reverend said, the M.D. was screaming in my ear at the time, but, whatever it was, it must have worked because Severn turned back to the microphone he was adjusting. The M.D. snorted like a draught horse and flounced offstage.

The Reverend was still kneeling on the floor, talking quietly to Severn at the microphone when Seth burst up the stairs, demanding to know what was going on. I started to explain but he pushed past me, grabbed Severn by his shirt front and hauled him to his feet.

"Keep out of it!" he snarled a warning to the Reverend before the smaller man had a chance to open his mouth.

"Don't push your luck any more, Jura." Seth gave Severn a bone-rattling shake. "And if you've got a problem with me, or with Aiden or Meredith, you deal with us, don't take it out on the mor... on the members of the society."

Severn stumbled backwards as Seth let go. A fake street lamp stopped him from falling. He leant against it, breathing heavily for a few seconds then he straightened up and walked determinedly back to Seth.

"I don't have a problem with you," he replied coldly. "Unless it was you who moved the microphone. I have a problem with an idiot musician."

Seth glared at him. Something was happening between them that I didn't understand. For a minute I thought Seth was going to argue, or even hit him, but he didn't. He just gave Severn a shove like he was reminding him who was boss, then he backed off. The Reverend let out a deep sigh and said nothing.

And just then, Tasha arrived. Spot on bad timing. I loved it.

She flounced up and grabbed Severn by the arm.

"Ah, there you are," she simpered, managing the patented Tasha bottom-wiggle-and-chest-upthrust manoeuvre as she spoke.

Severn looked down slowly, his eyes narrowing dangerously as he carefully removed her hands from his arm. He paused before answering in a tone so cold you could have ice-skated on it.

"Tasha, get out of my face!"

It was the best thing I'd heard all day.

CHAPTER EIGHT

I left Tasha standing centre stage, gobsmacked. It seemed the only right place to be at the moment was outside the theatre, out in the daylight. Matinees are weird that way. It's so dark in the theatre, especially backstage, and usually you are there at night so it's dark outside as well. But with matinees you walk out of the door and into another world. There are people everywhere, shopping, talking and driving by, and it's so bright. The sun is shining. That's the weirdest thing. After hours in the dark the brightness almost hurts.

I squinted up my eyes into the sunlight and turned from the end of the alley towards the little street of old-fashioned shops opposite the theatre entrance. The street was historic and had recently been closed to traffic by the city council to allow the coffee bars and restaurants to set their tables up outside. Now it was full of little tourist shops crammed with expensive and rare items that I could never afford. I wandered past the lady's lingerie shop and tried to imagine what some of the slinky, silky pieces would feel like to wear. Then I imagined what they would look like on my round-in-all-the-wrong-places body and moved on hurriedly. As I approached the shop that sold antique jewellery, I realised Olivia and Meredith were standing in the doorway, looking in the windows. Olivia was still wearing her medieval creation and Meredith had changed into something similar, although hers was dark green. Both were wearing dark glasses and huge felt hats with large floppy brims.

"Oh look," Olivia was saying in her quaint, high-pitched, sing-songy voice. "It's got a broken wing. It can't fly. Poor little sparrow, all broken. Can't fly, can't fly."

"Can't fly, can't fly," Meredith joined her in a chant that sounded like little school children in a playground. Then her tone changed. "Lucky for it, then. Little sparrows that learn to fly just get eaten by great, big hawks!" The last three words were stressed in a nasty voice like a child would say "big, scary witch", complete with talon-like moves with her hands. Then they saw me, giggled like little girls and ran off down the street, hand in hand, laughing and chanting "can't fly, can't fly".

I was totally bemused. I mean, they're adults, right? Yet they sounded and acted like kids of five or six. It didn't make any sense. I stopped to look in the jewellery shop window to see what they had been talking about. Amongst the collection of old rings and watches lay a tiny bluebird on a chain. There was a crack across the blue porcelain of its body and one wing-tip had been broken off. The price tag had a huge "reduced" sign on it. The bird looked sad.

I stared at the various items in the window for a few minutes, my gaze returning frequently to the little injured bird. I knew how it felt. Out of place amongst all the flash stuff, it reminded me of myself, with my Australian accent and not-so-thin body, out of place amongst the trendy, been-together-since-kindergarten group I went to school with. I made a rash decision, hauled my wallet out of my back pocket and strode into the shop. A few moments later, the little bird secured around my neck, I headed back to the theatre to prepare for the second show.

By the time I returned Olivia and Meredith had already changed out of their dresses back into black trousers and sweatshirts and were hard at work moving scenery into place. I couldn't figure out how they had got back and got changed so fast, especially as they had run off in the opposite direction to the theatre, but I didn't have time to think about it too deeply as Beth grabbed my arm and dragged me off to help her with the park bench. Later I was to add it to all the little things that didn't make sense until it was too late.

I saw Mum and Grant arrive back while I was setting the bench so as soon as the task was completed I hurried off to Mum's dressing room. I've learned from experience that doing the right, daughterly thing can reap rewards and I was right - she had brought me coke and a bag of barbeque flavoured Pringles. She wanted to sit and have a meaningful talk about Dad's proposal that I go to Australia but I managed to keep her off the subject till it was too late. The thirty minute call came over the dressing room speakers and Mum had to start her vocal warm-ups so I was able to grab my chips and dash to the safety of the scenery dock.

The stage door was open when I reached the dock so I wandered out to put my now empty chip container into the rubbish skip. I threw in the Pringles container and slammed the lid then grabbed a few last gasps of fresh air and rays of sunshine before wandering slowly back into the gloom of the dock. As my eyes adjusted to the dark I saw Tasha and the other dancers strutting their way across the stage, waggling their red feathers.

My mind played a bizarre memory trick. I saw the dancers strutting, Mum hacking that casserole chicken and heard Olivia and Meredith chant "Can't fly, can't fly."

"Nasty things feathers. Make a right mess."

"What the ...? Where did you come from?" I exclaimed, startled, as Finn appeared beside me, pushing a large broom and carrying several of the dancers' moulted red feathers. He laughed softly, touching his finger to his nose in a gesture that said "my secret". I muttered something unintelligible and turned away, my heart pounding. Had he read my mind? Where had he materialised from? He had certainly made no noise arriving. I took a deep breath and pulled myself together.

There were now only fifteen minutes to go till show time, the audience was starting to fill the seats and the dancers should not have been anywhere near the stage. It gave me a sense of power to be able to order them off the stage and into the wings and Tasha's catty remarks and evil glare didn't phase me at all, especially as Severn caught the whole thing from where he was checking microphones in the corner. He gave me a wicked grin and a thumbs-up sign which turned to two raised fingers to Tasha's retreating plumed behind.

The second show seemed to fly past with hardly any mistakes, partly due to the extra effort everyone was putting in to make sure they weren't the one to screw up and partly because of the S.M.'s dire threats of revenge on anyone who did. Plus, it was Saturday night and everyone, cast and crew, was looking forwards to the first real party of the season.

CHAPTER NINE

One of the good things about parties is seeing the sides of people they don't normally show. Like teachers getting drunk. Dilly Davenport became quite entertaining as the evening wore on.

I had changed out of my crew blacks, not because I didn't like wearing them, quite the opposite. But I knew they had to survive one more show before I could spare them to the washing machine and I also knew that, with my luck, I'd spill something on them that wouldn't sponge off. So as soon as we arrived home after the evening performance, I ducked off to my room and swapped them for a white t-shirt and a long grape-coloured skirt. To finish it off, I threw on my white muslin shirt and my Doc Marten eight-hole cherry reds.

Ok, I know what you're thinking. Riley Lowe in a skirt? Yeah, well, it happens sometimes, when I'm in the mood. And, let's be honest here, if you were in my situation and faced with a male with the most gorgeous eyes you've ever seen and a predatory Tasha, wouldn't you use any ammunition at your disposal? I mean, he's only ever seen me in black jeans that make my backside rival the one on the horse that carts the Japanese tourists around the Square and he's so slim. I had to do something!

For most of the evening, though, I thought my careful planning had all been in vain. The Borman crew was a no-show. Part of me was really disappointed and the other half decided on a conscious effort not to care. Who was he anyway? So what? But when Mum asked me if "my sound man" was coming and I just shrugged and muttered "I don't know", I don't think she was fooled at all.

I think what made it worse was that Tasha didn't notice that Severn wasn't there. She was having plenty of fun flirting with the horde of panting young chorus men. And with Jason Broderick.

I must admit, I got pretty hooked watching this part of the action.

Jason Broderick is your classic tall, dark, handsome type, the sort that gets lead roles on afternoon soap operas. He'd already been a guest villain on "Shortland Street". He's twenty eight. I know that because I overheard Grant and some of the committee members talking when they were hiring him. That makes him twelve years older than Tasha and about a hundred years younger than Dilly Davenport. Well, okay, about five years but teachers are all prehistoric. Even if he was nearer my age, I still wouldn't fancy him. It would be like going out with a walkie-talkie Ken doll. I guess that made him an ideal target for Tasha the Barbie clone.

And she certainly targeted him. From the moment he made his late but strategically planned entrance, she was straight in like an exocet missile. I'll swear she's got a radar beacon built into the underwiring in her bra. They made a perfect couple. He posed and flashed his perfect white teeth and she laughed in carefully modulated tones at all his pathetic jokes.

That was about when Dilly Davenport started sinking back Grant's cheap sparkling white supermarket wine by the pint glass. Then the competition began.

Dilly had more theatrical experience, so she knew how to command an audience. Her voice became louder, her hand movements more extravagant. Everybody, including me, became "Darling" and "Sweetie" and every man who came within grabbing distance was hauled around the floor in a quick tango or a slow waltz.

Tasha was not to be outdone. It took only one eyelash bat to convince one of her panting horde to change the cd and it was Tasha's turn on the floor in a reckless display of the latest dance steps. Dilly sank another wine and took up the challenge, matching her step for step. She may be a teacher but, I'll give her one thing, that woman can dance. Jason clapped but I wasn't sure who it was for.

I was so busy watching the battle, I didn't notice the others until the computer froze. Grant had taken a couple of his friends into his office to play on his new toy or to "surf the net" as he insisted on calling it. But he'd done something wrong and the whole machine had locked up. He came out looking sheepish and made a general announcement to the room asking if anyone knew how to fix computers. I only realised Severn was there when I heard his distinctive voice ask "hardware or software?" It was another hour before I got to talk to him.

By that time most of the party had gone home to get some sleep and only the hardiest party-goers were still slugging it out in the lounge. Tasha had been carried off by an attentive horde member after being horribly sick in the front garden. Mum was still playing the hostess but I could tell by the look in her eyes that she just wished they would all leave.

I thought a cup of coffee could be a good idea but the kitchen was in use. Dilly and Jason were locked hips and lips and he was muttering about how she, presumably Tasha, didn't mean anything and how she, presumably Dilly, was all he wanted. I backed off, leaving them to it and headed towards my room, running straight into Grant and Severn as they finally emerged from Grant's office. Severn smiled.

"Join us for coffee?" Grant inquired.

"I was just going to make some but the kitchen's...um...taken," I faltered.

Grant got the hint and laughed. He swung towards the kitchen door, making as much noise as possible. The ploy worked as Dilly and Jason were casually reading the review by the time we walked into the room. They excused themselves quickly and left. Grant put the electric jug on to boil then asked if I'd take over while he went to find Mum.

Can I help? Severn asked shyly.

"Yeah, grab some mugs," I said, pointing in the direction of the cupboards.

Severn found four and brought them to the bench where he put them down in front of me.

"I'm sorry I didn't speak to you today," he began.

"It's okay," I said, a bit embarrassed. "You sounded like you were having a bad day."

"Yes," Severn gave a self-depreciating laugh. "You could say that. But I had no right to take it out on you. I'm sorry. Am I forgiven?"

I nodded, mumbled and risked looking up into his eyes. The smile was gone, replaced with a gentle, serious expression. Without any more words, he put his arms around me and pulled me to him. I closed my eyes and relaxed into the strength of his body, the warm rush of his breath against my face and the heady rush as his lips came down on mine.

A warm tingle ran down my spine as his firm grasp drew my body hard against his. With a small groan of pleasure, I let my lips part in invitation to his questing tongue.

He kissed me long and hard, then pulled away with a gentle smile.

"This is not getting the coffee made," he said softly.

"No, it isn't," I replied.

Both his statement and my reply were stupid but it was one of those moments when you know you have to say something to bring things back to normal, so anything will do. But things weren't back to normal. For one thing, his hands were still locked firmly around my waist and for another, mine were locked just as tightly around his.

Under my fingers I could feel two hard muscles running up his back, one on either side of his spine. I wasn't thinking about coffee as I let my fingers touch them again. He shivered slightly under my touch and moved his hands to move mine to his hips.

"Don't touch me there, please," he whispered.

I wanted to ask why but he put his fingers to my lips to stop me asking.

"Don't ask about things I don't want to explain." He spoke softly and was just about to distract me from asking more with another kiss when there was a noise in the hallway. We leapt apart just as Seth Borman surged through the kitchen door.

"We're leaving now!" he ordered.

"What's the hurry," said Severn calmly, smiling at me as he did do.

"We're hungry," Seth replied sharply, as if that was Severn's fault.

"So go eat."

"Don't get smart!" Seth did not sound amused and I was very aware yet again that there was something really deep going on between them that I did not understand. "We are hungry, we are leaving and you are supplying the food," he continued menacingly.

"What if I'm not ready to leave," Severn challenged.

"Yeah," I butted in. "Why does Severn have to run after you lot? Can't you cook for yourselves?"

Seth began to say something but Severn stepped between us, his back to Seth, his hands on my shoulders.

"Stay out," he said gently. Then he turned to Seth. "She does have a point though. Why can't one of you...ah...shop for a change?"

"It's your job." The coldness of Seth's reply suggested no other reason was required.

"So! That doesn't mean David, or Aiden, couldn't go for once." I was quick to notice Severn's use of the Reverend's real name.

"All right. Have it your way!" Seth pulled back his lips in a nasty little smile. "I'll send the girls."

"No!" Severn's reply was almost a shout. "No!" Then he seemed to give up. "Ok," he shrugged. "Go home and I'll meet you there. I'll bring you breakfast in bed." He delivered the last part with lots of sarcasm and I had a quick mental picture of Dylan Thomas's play "Under Milkwood" where the husband brings his nagging wife a pot of arsenic tea and a weedkiller biscuit.

"Don't be long," Seth snarled as he spun on his heel and left.

Beside me, Severn sighed.

"Looks like I'll have to go," he said sadly. I'll see you tomorrow." Then he planted a small kiss on my forehead and followed his boss out the door.

By the time Mum and Grant had come through, I had the coffee made and some biscuits on a plate. I didn't know if the fact that I had been kissing Severn showed. I hoped not.

If it did they didn't mention it, although Mum smiled as if she knew.

Later, I lay in bed and thought about the evening. About Tasha, about Dilly Davenport and her drunken dancing and about Severn. I thought lots about Severn.

It wasn't like he was the first person I'd kissed. He was just the best.

As I turned over to flick off my bedside light, I patted my huge stuffed white rabbit that used to go to bed with me when I was little and who now spent its time sitting on a pile of unwashed laundry beside the bed.

"Tasha dipped out," I told it smugly. "She didn't get Jason Broderick, she didn't get Severn. Oh dear. How sad. What a nice day."

CHAPTER TEN

"Did Tasha know she'd been unsuccessful with both these men?" The woman policeman stepped forwards as she asked the question.

I shrugged.

"I don't know about Jason, but she didn't know about Severn. Not on Saturday anyway."

"What makes you so sure?"

"I told you that already! She'd been carried off long before then, she got so drunk she passed out."

"Did she know Severn was at the party?"

"No, she couldn't have." I thought carefully. "Like I said before, I didn't know he was there until the computer broke down. If she'd seen him she would have been all over him, just to piss me off, and I think I would've noticed that."

"So you are reasonably certain that when Tasha left your house on Saturday night, or early Sunday morning, she did not know she was not wanted by either man?" the cop repeated.

"As far as I know," I answered truthfully.

"And later on Sunday? Did she know then?"

"I don't know, she might have done."

"You didn't tell her?"

"No, why should I? "

"Temptation, Miss Lowe," the male cop butted in, his body leaning forwards threateningly over the desk towards me, his pen thrust menacingly into my face. "Temptation. You didn't want to gloat, by any chance?"

"No," I said indignantly. "Well, not on Sunday anyway. I left that till Monday at school."

"But you did have a show on Sunday," the cop phrased it as a statement, not a question.

"Yes, a late matinee at four o'clock. It wasn't very good though, most us were too tired or hung-over. The stage manager should have been cross with everyone, but she wasn't any better herself."

"How was Tasha?"

"Sick as a dog," I laughed. "She had a rotten headache and was sick in the toilet at least twice."

"And Severn?"

"He was okay. Well, sort of okay. I didn't get to see him much, just for a couple of minutes at interval. I tried to see him before the show but Seth had him up in the fly tower re-rigging some cables and after the show Aiden dragged him away to do something. I thought he looked really tired."

"Tired? Is that all?"

"Well," I searched for the right words. He seemed really on edge. While we were talking at interval he kept fidgeting and looking over his shoulder as if he expected someone to come up behind him, and he wouldn't go out into the alley. No, it was obvious the cop was leading somewhere I didn't want to go and I wasn't prepared to help him get there. Besides. I wanted to go home. "Yeah, tired, " I nodded affirmatively. "He looked tired. We were all tired. In fact, I'm tired now, would you just tell me what this is all about so I can go home and sleep? I don't think you can keep me here anyway."

The cop sat back in his chair and stretched. He looked tired too.

"You're right, Miss Lowe, I can't keep you. However just one or two more questions?"

"Shoot," I shrugged, resigned.

"I just want to go over Sunday again. You barely talked to Severn and you didn't talk to Natasha?"

"Correct"

"Before the show?"

"No, we were running a bit late. Grant had to help the neighbour catch her dog. It had got out and was running up and down the street."

"Not even on the telephone later that evening?"

"No, why should I have? Look, like I said, we were all tired. We did the show and we left. Grant wanted to catch the news on tv to see if there was anything about that dead body you guys found on New Brighton beach, Mum wanted to do the laundry and visit the neighbour and I had a pile of homework to do."

"You said you kept your gloating till Monday at school," the female cop broke in. "Could you tell us about that."

I shrugged. "Tasha was doing her usual, playing centre stage to anyone who would listen. She was raving on to the others about Jason, saying what a hunk he was and she kept calling him 'my Jason'. 'My Jason this, my Jason that'. I got to the point where I couldn't stand it anymore so I pointed out that he didn't look much like 'her' Jason when he was in the kitchen snogging Dilly. The others all laughed and Tasha stormed off in a huff. Then the others wanted to know what I had seen so I told them and added that Tasha wouldn't know because she had already been carted off wasted.

"So," the cop tapped his pen again, "by Monday you felt you had exacted suitable revenge but Natasha now had reason to be angry with you for making her look like a fool in front of her peers."

"I guess so."

"And Severn? Did you see him on Monday?"

"There was no show on Monday. Or Tuesday." I knew I wasn't answering the question but I didn't want to have to explain.

"That didn't answer the question, Miss Lowe."

Damn!

"I did not speak to Severn on Monday, or Tuesday." My answer was worded very carefully. It was correct. I hadn't spoken to him. I had seen him but I didn't want to tell them that because I hadn't come to terms with it myself. There were two possible answers for what I saw, one sensible, one ridiculous, both of them bad for me. So I wasn't going to tell the cops if I could help it.

Yes, I had seen Severn on Monday evening. He hadn't seen me. I had planned a quiet evening at home watching Buffy the Vampire Slayer on tv but Anita had invited me to watch Buffy and a video at her place so I had gone over to her place after school. It was nice. We sat, watched tv, ate chips, gossiped and talked about Tasha behind her back. Anita does wicked impersonations of Tasha and Dilly so we had a truly joyous evening of bitching and backstabbing.

I left for home just after ten o'clock. Anita lives on the other side of town to me so I needed to get a bus into the Square then another bus from the city centre to home and I didn't want to miss the last bus and get stranded. The Square at night is not exactly the safest place to be, especially on your own. I guess that was the main reason I didn't ride the bus all the way into the Square. I pulled the cord a couple of streets away and walked down the brightly lit nightclub strip towards the bus stop for the trip home. That was when I saw Severn.

He was coming out of one of the clubs. It was definitely him. I recognised him instantly, even though he was all dressed up in a fancy pin-striped Italian business suit. Seth and Meredith were just behind him, similarly dressed up. Meredith was back in the dark green velvet dress I had seen her wearing on Saturday and Seth had a suit that looked from a distance as though it may have been black velvet. It was certainly old fashioned and just a bit too tight over his bulging muscles. They had their arms around each other. So did Severn. He had his arm comfortably around the waist of the person beside him, the person had their head resting on his shoulder. That was the problem. The other person was unquestionable male.

I was stunned. This wasn't happening. I was not seeing Severn with a man. No way! I needed to talk to him so I followed, thinking I could catch him up when they reached their van, which I could see parked in the next block, but before we reached it they turned off, into an alleyway. I approached carefully and peeked around the edge of the building. Seth and Meredith were standing, arm in arm, watching as Severn embraced the man. I saw his head dip down in what looked like the beginnings of a passionate move and I heard Seth laugh. I wanted to turn and run but I was stuck fast, held in place by a mixture of curiosity and revulsion. Seth put a hand on Severn's shoulder, pulling him back.

"My turn." His deep voice echoed down the alley.

Severn stepped aside, rubbing his hand across his mouth, and Seth took his place, bending his head to the obviously drunk male.

I didn't stay any longer. I ran and ran, past the bus stop and on to the next one, anything to get as far away as possible. Later, in bed, I dreamed, a violent mixture containing Severn, Seth, Buffy and lots of small, featherless, dead birds. I woke with a start, shivering with fear. All I could think of was the two possibilities - the logical or the ridiculous. Either Severn and Seth were kissing the guy, in which case they were gay, or at least into some alternate sort of lifestyle that I didn't want to know about, or the ridiculous science fiction explanation – they weren't kissing him, they were biting him. They were vampires. The guy I fancied either fancied other men, or he killed and ate them. Some choice! A sensible, logical but I-don't-want-to-know-about–it answer, or a totally ridiculous, impossible, only-on-the-horror-movies answer. I lay there shivering, thinking it through till I came to a decision. After the delicious kiss I had shared at the party, I didn't want to believe the sensible answer so I went with the other. Vampires I could handle.

CHAPTER ELEVEN

"Tuesday, Miss Lowe. Did you see either of them yesterday?" The cop's insistent voice broke through my drifting thoughts. I pulled myself together quickly, rubbing my eyes and yawning to pretend I was just tired and not withholding information.

"Tasha. I saw Tasha at school. I didn't see Severn at all."

"What was Natasha like yesterday? Was she in a good mood?"

"Yeah. She was her normal catty, show-off self."

"Did you talk about the show?"

"No. Actually I didn't really talk to her at all. Our group kind of split up in to two. Somebody mentioned Shortland Street and Tasha managed to turn that around to Jason and the role he had played on it. According to her he was going to make a return but it was all supposed to be a secret. She acted like she was so special because she knew. Anita and I couldn't be bothered so we moved away and talked about Buffy instead and a couple of the others came with us."

"After school?"

"I went home. I had made a deal with Mum that I would iron the clothes we would need for tonight's show. Mum was washing some of the costumes so there was a bit of a pile to get through and Mum had offered me ten dollars to iron them for her." I wasn't going to tell him that I just wanted time on my own to think through what I had seen the night before and plan my tactics for when I next saw Severn.

"Where were you on Tuesday evening, Miss Lowe?"

"At home. Ironing clothes and watching tv."

"Who else was there?" The cop was starting to sound pretty insistent and I didn't like the way the questions were heading, like he thought I was guilty of something.

"Mum and Grant," I answered. He wrote that down. "And the neighbour, Mrs Greenaway. She came over to talk to Mum. They sat in the kitchen, drank coffee and talked about her stupid dog. Can I go home now?"

"Soon, Miss Lowe. Just tell me, what was Natasha like today?"

"Sick. She wasn't at school and she didn't turn up to the show. Dilly said she had come down with some kind of a bug and might not be there for a couple of days?"

"Were you told this at the theatre or at school?"

"At the theatre. We noticed she wasn't at school but we figured she was bunking. She did that often enough."

"So you weren't concerned? You didn't phone her house to ask?"

"Nope."

"So the last time you saw Natasha was yesterday at school?'

"Yep"

"You are certain of that?"

I sighed. "Yes." Then I started to click. "Hang on, what exactly is going on here?"

"You tell me, Miss Lowe. What do know about what happened at the theatre tonight?"

I breathed deeply and sat back in the hard, wooden chair.

"Everything was normal. We went to the theatre. I did my presets. No, before you ask, I didn't see Severn but then, I must admit I was hoping to stay out of his road. I did what I had to do and then visited Mum in her dressing room till they called beginners."

"When did you realise Natasha was not there?" the cop butted in.

"At the beginner's call when she didn't line up with the other dancers. I whispered to one of them to ask where she was and she told me what Dilly had said."

"Then what happened?"

"Nothing, at least for a while. Actually, I don't know what happened. The final song in Act One is the one when they use the rain truck."

"Explain that to me," the cop butted in again.

"For that scene it has to rain on stage. The set builders created this thing that is basically a giant shower tray the size of the stage. There is scenery on it to make it look like the rest of the set, it has two huge water tanks hidden behind the scenery and the whole thing is on wheels. At the scene change we all push like crazy and shove it into position then the mechanist pushes the switch and the pumps start and it rains. Then Jason sings his song on it, gets soaking wet and dashes off to dry off in the interval."

"Your job in this?"

"I help push it on and at the end of the scene I help push it back off again. All the crew do, it weighs about two tonnes when it's full with water."

"Who fills it?"

"The mechanist. It's part of his pre-set."

"How does he fill it? With a bucket? Does he pour the water in from the top?"

"No, that would take forever," I answered honestly. "It has a valve attached at the back. He's got a garden hose snaked up from the laundry downstairs and he just attaches it and turns it on. Turns it off when it's full."

"How does he know when it's full?" the cop inquired.

"There's a gauge on the side that shows you how much water is in it."

"So no-one would have needed to look inside before the show?"

"No." I shook my head firmly. What was he getting at?

"And tonight? Do you know what happened tonight?"

"No, not really. I think someone put red dye in the water because Jason was furious when he came off stage. He finished the song like everything was normal but when he came off he was dripping red water and there was red water in the gutterings when we pushed the truck back."

"What did you do then?"

"Nothing. I knew something was wrong because Seth climbed up to look in the tank then he, the stage manager and Grant went off into a corner to talk. Then the stage manager announced over the backstage system that there was a problem, however we had to do the second act and finish the show but we would all have to stay back afterwards. I tried to ask Grant what had happened but he just said he would tell me later then he rushed off somewhere. I asked Mum but she didn't know either. So we finished the show, everybody got changed, we all came back on stage and found you guys there. And you know as much about the rest of it as I do. You separated us all into groups and I guess you are asking everyone the same dumb questions you're asking me."

I paused and thought about that for a second or two.

"No, you let most people go home. You brought me down here and asked me all sorts of things about Tasha and Severn. I think you had better tell me exactly what is going on here."

"Where is Severn?"

The question surprised me.

"I don't know. With the rest of the crew I suppose."

"He's disappeared, Miss Lowe. We know he was at the show but sometime between the show finishing and our interviews, he has vanished. Do you know where he could have gone, Miss Lowe?"

"No, why should I? Why is it important anyway? Maybe he went out to get food? What's the big deal? Unless you think he is guilty of putting the dye in the rain truck."

"It wasn't dye, Miss Lowe. It was blood. Natasha Moreland's blood. She's not sick, Miss Lowe, she's dead. The object Seth found in the rain truck was her severed head."

CHAPTER TWELVE

"Where was the rest of her?" I asked when they finally let me out. The cop had wanted to "go over it again, from the beginning" but I made a big show of yawning and looking at my watch and he must have finally realised that it was nearly three in the morning.

"We'll leave it at that for now, Miss Lowe," he said pompously, "but we will need to talk to you again."

"Great," I replied sarcastically. "I can't wait."

"We will need her to make a formal statement," he told my mother as he delivered me to her in the hallway. "We will call you to make a suitable time."

"Mmm," Mum muttered a vague reply then drew me down to sit beside her on an uncomfortable vinyl coated bench that sat against the wall of the corridor. "They're still talking to Grant," she said in the sort of almost-whisper people use in doctor's waiting rooms.

"Don't worry," I told her. "They're not after him, they're after Severn."

"What?" Mum sounded genuinely horrified.

"I reckon. Apparently he disappeared when the show finished, so I guess in their book that makes him guilty."

"But that's ridiculous," Mum retorted. "That would be advertising that you were guilty. Whoever did it would know better than that. They would have stayed and tried to look as normal as possible. No, no, no. The real killer was probably standing beside us all the time."

As soon as she had said the words, Mum took in their meaning. Her hands flew to her mouth. "Oh no!" she exclaimed. "One of our theatre company is a murderer!"

"Not necessarily," I tried to sound more reassuring than I felt. "It could have been someone she knew from somewhere else. She could have taken them there. I will bet one thing, knowing Tasha, I'll bet it was a guy."

"Well it wasn't Grant and I wish they would let him go." Mum sounded panicky.

"Of course it wasn't. Nobody thinks it was. But he is the president of the society so it's obvious they will have a lot of questions for him."

"They kept you a long time. I was getting worried."

"Yeah, well, I was the one that knew Tasha best. Plus they seem to think I know a lot about Severn as well, which I don't. I'm sure they think I am hiding him somewhere."

"Are you?"

"Mother!"

"Sorry."

"Anyway,' I changed the topic to something that was beginning to fascinate me now that the initial horror had subsided. "If her head was in the rain truck, where was the rest of her?"

Mum paused a long time before replying.

"Seth found her, down in the hole in the floor where the fly counterweights drop." She paused again. "She wasn't wearing any knickers."

"Oh," I started to giggle. "I guess that shortens the odds on my bet that it must have been a guy."

At that moment a door opened further down the corridor and Grant appeared. He had worn old track pants and a paint-stained sweatshirt into the theatre and by now, tired and with a few hours growth on his whiskers, he looked like a homeless tramp. Mum leapt to her feet and rushed to him.

"Let's go home," he said as they hugged.

"Wait for me, I need to go to the ladies," I said quickly as we headed towards the lifts.

"They're up on the next floor," Mum said, pointing to the stairs. "We'll wait for you here."

I hurried up the stairs to find the toilets so I was alone when I past a door and heard Severn's name mentioned. I stopped to listen.

"It was the name, it rang a bell," I heard a male voice say. "It's funny, it was a few years ago now but I thought of it the other day when that body turned up on New Brighton beach. Now with this business, well, I did some checking."

"You're telling me that Severn Jura has a record?" I recognised the voice of the cop who had interviewed me. "Tell me all about it."

"Like I said, it was a few years ago now, in Dunedin. A body was found at the Taieri river mouth. It had the same marks as the one found at New Brighton, that's what made me think of him. We found a card in the dead guy's pocket with an address and a set of fingerprints. Both led us to a guy called Severn Jura. He admitted knowing the guy and giving him the card but we could never pin anything on him so eventually we had to let the matter drop and he disappeared. We lost track of him and the case ended up in the unsolved pile."

"Thanks, Bob, once again your prodigious memory for trivial facts is put to good use."

"There's another fact you may not like."

"Yes?"

"Like I said, this was a few years ago, a rather long time ago. How old would you say Jura is?"

"Eighteen, nineteen at the most."

"Hmm, that's the problem. Jura was listed as nineteen then and I was twenty two. I retire later this year. The case was over forty years ago, Jura should be pushing sixty if he's a day."

"So? Maybe this one's his son, or grandson even?"

"This is the bit you're not going to like. I said there were fingerprints on the card. I checked. They match the prints we took off Jura's sound board this evening. They are exactly the same. By all accounts, it's the same guy."

CHAPTER THIRTEEN

I let Mum and Grant do all the talking on the way home. Fortunately Mum got all maternal and decided it had all been too stressful for me and I should just be allowed to go to sleep, both in the car and once we arrived home, so I didn't have to join in their frantic speculations. I didn't even listen to them as my mind was spinning with odd thoughts but I did take in one thing Grant said. Apparently the mechanist had reported finding the fire door at the back of the dressing rooms unbolted and carefully left so it looked shut but could have been opened easily from the outside. Grant thought that widened the field and proved it didn't have to be a member of the theatre company as anyone could have got in, but Mum argued exactly the opposite - it had to have been an inside job to have known about the door, let alone unbolt it.

I left them to their discussion and crawled off to bed and when I woke it was mid-morning and the lounge was full of theatre company committee in an emergency meeting. I made myself some toast with marmalade and sneaked in to listen.

The debate was becoming heated. One half of the committee thought the show should be closed immediately. They argued that the whole matter would be splurged all over tonight's news and that carrying on singing and dancing when a member of the troupe had died horribly was in extremely bad taste. The other half thought we should carry on but Grant should make a formal statement before tonight's show dedicating it to Tasha. They argued that she would have preferred the show to go on. They also argued on the grounds of money. The show was costing thousands of dollars to stage and if we closed only a few days after opening the company would not be able to pay its debts. The ones who wanted to close said continuing was morbid and only ghouls would come out of some sick curiosity and the others argued that who cared why they came as long as they bought tickets and we got their money. Mum, surprisingly, was voting for continuing and Grant, as usual, dithered.

Even though I'm not on the committee, I spoke up to say that I agreed with the idea of Grant dedicating the show to Tasha. I knew exactly how much she liked to be the centre of attention and I figured she would be loving it. Besides, I didn't want the show to end. In a really childish way I didn't want her to spoil my fun again. Ever since I had arrived at Eastgate High she had always managed to spoil everything that I enjoyed. When we went on school camps she wore designer clothes and complained when they got dirty. When our class went skiing she twisted her ankle and made the ski instructor carry her back down the slope. In a way she was doing it again. Anyone else would have died quietly of pneumonia or something. Trust Tasha to be spectacularly murdered. I wanted to finish the show because I was enjoying it. I also wanted to find Severn.

The argument went backwards and forwards for another hour but ended abruptly when Grant received two phone calls in quick succession. The first was from the police telling him that there was no way the theatre could be opened to the public tonight as they would still be carrying out forensic inquiries; the second was from Tasha's mother saying she hoped the show would continue as she knew Tasha would not have wanted it to close. Armed with that information, Grant declared that the show would open again on Friday and would carry on as normal for the rest of the run. There were murmurings of "ghouls" and "disgusting" but when a vote was called for, Grant's motion was passed by two votes and the meeting broke up.

Mum invited a select few of her friends to stay for lunch. I helped her rustle up some thick soup and herb bread and we spent another couple of hours going over everybody's recollections of the previous night and their experiences with the police inquiry team. Grant had the most to say and I tried to stay out of it until Mum volunteered the information that I had spent ages talking to the police and that apparently Severn was a prime suspect. Of course that got everyone's attention and I had to tell them every little detail of my hours at the police station. It didn't help my temper that as soon as school finished Anita arrived at the door wanting to know what had happened and I realised I would have to tell the story all over again. Muttering curses, I dragged her off to my room to swap notes.

"So what's going on?" she asked breathlessly, flinging her jacket and backpack into the corner.

"What do you think is going on?" I was being cautious.

"Well, something sure is." She made herself comfortable on the edge of my bed. "You weren't at school today, Tasha hasn't been there since Monday, even Miss Davenport is away."

"Maybe we're all sick and it's really serious and now you're here, you'll catch it too."

"Maybe chocolate fish can swim!" She didn't believe me. "Maybe you'll tell me why there were police outside the theatre last night when the show finished." Anita could tell by my expression that she had hit home. "Jo told us, in theatre arts. She went to see it last night and said there were cop cars everywhere afterwards. Jonathon Carter reckons that's why Dilly wasn't in class. He said she'd probably been arrested for drugs or something." She paused, obviously waiting for me to speak. I told her the truth.

She sat, stunned, for several seconds, her mouth hanging open like a fish, then she leapt off the bed, grabbed the telephone extension by my bed and started dialling. From the rapid way she fired the information down the line to friends, I figured at least half the town would know about it long before it broke on the tv news.

"It must have been sooo gruesome," she gushed as she finished her last call. "Imagine. Cutting her head off. Think of all the blood!"

"Yeah, whatever." I replied, borrowing the reply Severn uses when he can't be bothered with what you are saying. I wasn't going to share it with Anita but while she was speaking I had been imagining the scene backstage and a few random snatches of conversation had clicked together in my head. I had an idea but to test it I would have to get into the theatre.

CHAPTER FOURTEEN

I figured I would have to wait till well after midnight. I didn't know how late the forensic team would stay at the theatre and I didn't want to get caught. I also didn't want Mum or Grant to find out so I wanted to make sure they were well and truly asleep. Fortunately I wasn't tired as I had slept so late, so it was easy enough to stay awake. I watched tv with them, catching as many news broadcasts across the various channels as we could. Obviously they share resources as the film footage was always the same - the outside of the theatre showing a poster of our show, an interview with Jason Broderick who said it was all "simply frightful", and a tearful interview with Tasha's mother in which she showed photos of Tasha in various skimpy dance costumes with fancy silver trophies. Grant's official statement from the theatre company which displayed carefully worded horror and sadness at the brutal death of "a young and vibrant member of the troupe" but which stressed that "in accordance with the wishes of her family the show would go on," was read by a reporter as Grant had refused to be drawn into what he termed the "media circus".

They went to bed at about eleven thirty and I made a cheap excuse about making myself some drinking chocolate so they wouldn't think it was strange if I didn't follow straight away. I actually did make myself the drink, and some toast, and took them down to my room where I turned on my stereo softly and settled down with a book to fill in the time.

It was almost one o'clock when I heard a noise at my window. At first I thought it was the tree which Grant has never got around to trimming, but when it continued, I pulled back the curtain and stared straight into the distraught face of Severn.

He motioned me to keep quiet but the warning was unnecessary, I was already easing the window catch to let him in.

"The police are looking for you," I whispered as he sat, shivering, on the end of my bed. "You look frozen." That just goes to show how stupid I can be. I mean, it's midnight, I have just let into my bedroom the man who may have cut off my friend's head and I am worrying because he looks cold.

"I am," he acknowledged, rubbing the bare arms that protruded from the lightweight t-shirt.

I rummaged quickly in my drawers and found him a hooded

sweatshirt then threw him the extra blanket I keep in my wardrobe for really cold nights.

"The police are looking for you," I repeated.

"I know. So is Seth. I can't let either of them find me. Can I hide here tonight?"

'Umm," I hesitated, my brain processing quick scenarios of Mum walking in.

"I won't hurt you." Severn looked pleadingly from the folds of the blanket. "I didn't kill her."

"I know," I replied. "I never thought you did. I'm just worried that here isn't a very safe place to hide. It's a bit obvious isn't it?"

"Just for tonight. Please? I won't be any bother. I'm cold, I'm tired and I'm very hungry. I just want to warm up and rest for a while and if you've got any food I'd really appreciate it. I also need to find a way to get a message to David, to the Reverend, without Seth and the others finding out. I thought I might have been able to sneak into the show but the only people there tonight were police."

"You went there? You've been to the theatre?" I was horrified.

"Yes. I was careful. Don't forget, I was trying to avoid Seth. You have to be really careful to do that. If I can avoid him, I can certainly avoid the police."

"Maybe." I wasn't convinced. "Look, stay here and I'll go and find some food. Then we'll talk."

Leaving him behind, I made my way quietly to the kitchen. Luckily the lounge and kitchen are in the middle of our house with the main bedrooms at the front while my bedroom is all by itself at the back. That's why I chose it. So I was able to make a huge pile of toast and two mugs of coffee without disturbance. I carried the mugs and plate carefully back to my bedroom, placed them on the dresser and, as Severn ate ravenously, I plied him with questions.

"Why the Reverend? Why is he any more trustworthy than the others? Why are they after you? Come to that, if you didn't kill Tasha why did you run away? If you ran away before we found out she was dead, how did you know there was anything to run away from, unless you really did do it and if you did I am now in very deep shit." I faded off wishing I had stopped talking several sentences earlier.

Severn pulled the blanket tighter around himself and sighed.

"I said it before and I meant it, I didn't kill Tasha, even though she was a silly cow and she probably deserved all she got. See, now I've even given you a motive so you can join all the others and think the worst. I think she was one of the most irritating, up-herself people I have ever met, Seth included, and I am not sorry that someone got so fed up with her that they chopped her head off. They probably did it to stop her talking. But, I repeat, I did not hate her enough to kill her. That would take energy that she was not worth expending. I did, however, know that she was dead, long before you did. We all did. Yes, I know you all think that Seth found her during the interval, but that isn't strictly true. David found her earlier in the evening, when we first arrived. We just chose not to say anything."

"What?" I squeaked. "You guys knew Tasha was dead, inside the rain truck, and you didn't tell anyone? Why?"

Severn shrugged.

"It wasn't our problem. None of us were responsible. We didn't do it and we didn't want all the hassle. I mean, if you find a body you're automatically a suspect and we didn't need that sort of strife. We figured she was one of you and you people could sort it out."

"So why did you run away? That only made the police assume you were guilty. Isn't that just creating the hassle you just said you didn't want?"

He shrugged again.

"I guess. But I didn't run because of her. I ran to save my own skin. If Seth catches me, I'm dead."

CHAPTER FIFTEEN

Try as I might, I couldn't get Severn to explain any more. He agreed he and Seth didn't get along with each other but when I suggested that he quit the group and find another job somewhere else, he shook his head and said that was out of the question. When I asked why, he refused to say anything and it's not possible to argue with someone who doesn't answer. In the end I gave up and left him to finish the food.

He seemed surprised when I started putting on my jacket.

"Where are you going?"

"To the theatre. I want to have a look round."

"Are you sure that's safe?"

"No, but I'm going to do it anyway."

"Why?"

"Because I want to look at something."

"Ok, I'll come with you."

"No you won't. You are wanted by the police, remember? If I get caught I'm just being nosy, if you get caught, we're both history. Anyway, you said you were tired. You stay here, I'll be back in about an hour."

I checked my pockets - I had my maglight and Grant's theatre key that I had borrowed from its hook in the kitchen - then I let myself quietly out of the back door, expressing thanks that the neighbour's usually noisy dog was safely tucked away inside, grabbed my bike and pedalled furiously towards the city centre.

There is one thing I don't like about the theatre our company uses for its big shows - the area of town it is in, especially at night. It's on a street full of takeaway shops and right next door to the theatre is the biggest of the city's games arcades. It's not so bad during the day but as soon as it gets dark anybody human disappears fast and the block is taken over by rival gangs and the tarty girls who hang out with them. The theatre crew sometimes get hassled by the gangs because they think that anyone in black clothes must be a skinhead. We usually have the show's logo on our t-shirts but I guess gang members don't read too well. They can't be too smart, either, because most of the guys on the crew have muscles and you'd have to be really dumb to pick on someone who's just hoisted several tonnes of equipment into place with his bare hands.

But right now I was on my own with no hefty crew guys to save me, so I wasn't taking any chances. I biked quickly into the alley and hid my bike behind the rubbish skip, then I walked as quietly as I could back down the alley till I found the special little door that only Grant and the Theatre Manager had a key to. Feeling a bit like an actress in a spy movie, I checked up and down the alley guiltily before turning the key in the lock and gently opening the door.

I stepped onto the plush carpet of the richly curtained corridor that funnels audience from the foyer into the theatre itself, turned and carefully closed the door behind me.

Listening for any sounds of police, I felt my way through the darkened theatre and up onto the stage. Once I was backstage I felt safer and switched on my tiny torch. My first stop was Tasha's dressing room. She shared it with about ten others so I certainly didn't expect to find anything like a note from the killer written in lipstick on the mirror, but that wasn't what I was after. I sat on one of the hard wooden make-up stools for a while getting my bearings then wandered through to the communal bathroom. I was right. The fire exit door was where I expected it to be but by the powdery marks on it, the police forensic team had got there before me. I guessed what they had found. I wandered through the dressing rooms, rummaged through racks of costumes, pocketed a piece of paper I found in one of them and left.

My next stop was the other side of the stage. I shone my torch down into the hole in the floor where Tasha's body had been found. The ropes and pulleys were stained red with dried blood and flecks of what I suspected were, but sincerely hoped were not, pieces of flesh. I noted with a strange detachment that I didn't feel sick or even emotional at the sight.

My final stop was the fly tower itself. It's a long haul up the huge ladder and it is strictly out of bounds for anyone except the flymen. Once or twice the stage manager or the mechanist has caught an actor climbing the ladder but the humiliation of having the stage manager screaming at them in front of their friends is usually enough to ensure they never do it a second time. I had never been up there and, in all honesty, I hadn't wanted to. Looking up from the bottom is enough to put me off. I hated to think what it would be like at the top. I was about to find out.

Gripping my torch in my teeth, I climbed slowly and determinedly, trying not to think about how far it was to the ground, till after what seemed like an eternity, I reached the relative safety of the tiny wooden platform. Grateful for the meagre handrail, I edged my way carefully along the platform till I had a full view of the stage. It was amazing. Down below, with my eyes now accustomed to the dark, I could see the set like a tiny dollshouse below me. The twin tanks of the rain truck stared up at me like giant unseeing eyes and all around me was a plethora of hemp and wire ropes. It was like being in the rigging of a sailing ship and all of a sudden the mechanist's stories of how early theatres used sailors on shore leave as riggers made perfect sense. The fear of being so high up eased away and I started to enjoy myself. Maybe I'll talk to the mechanist about working flys in the next show - if they would let a girl have a try.

Still thinking about that, I scurried easily back down the ladder and hurried back through the theatre to the little door. I was just in time. As I approached, I froze as the main stage door opened and the distinct sound of a male voice echoed in the empty building.

"The lavender, third from the right. The bulb's blown, we'll replace it and refocus the side spots."

Seth!

I remembered Severn wanted to get a message to the Reverend. Maybe this would be my chance. I decided to hide and watch.

The heavy velvet curtains that marked the theatre entrances pleated themselves into huge folds where they met the aisles so it wasn't hard to sink onto my hands and knees and crawl through the pleats into the back row of seats and then along to the gap in the centre where seats had been removed to make room for Severn's large sound desk. From there I could peek through the seats and see what was happening. I didn't expect what I saw.

Seth was directing operations from the centre of the stage but it was Aiden and the Reverend who had my attention. I wathced mesmerised as both men stripped to the waist, dropping their clothes in untidy piles on the stage floor. In a few seconds they were high up in the lighting grid directly above Seth, Aiden holding the gel frame of a light and the Reverend replacing its bulb, but they were not on the wooden fly floor and they were not on the huge A-frame ladder. They were hanging in mid-air, suspended in place by the rhythmic flapping of their huge wings.

CHAPTER SIXTEEN

I couldn't describe the feelings that held me riveted in place. I wasn't terrified, I wasn't revolted, to be honest I wasn't even surprised. It felt unreal, like I was watching a video. I half expected Buffy the Vampire Slayer to leap down from the flys at any minute and jab one of the props walking sticks through Seth's ribcage. Come to think of it, that wouldn't be such a bad idea. I wasn't scared. I wasn't panicking. I was surprisingly calm, all things considered.

When a sudden, overwhelming urge to breathe made me realise that for the last minute or so, I hadn't, I gave in and admitted to myself that I was scared stiff. I was crouched as small as I could make myself behind the seats, peering through a gap between two chairs, my hands clamped tightly over my mouth to smother what I recognised was an overpowering desire to scream and I really needed to breathe. I let the air out as slowly as I could, in case my breath would be enough to give myself away, or in case once I started I wouldn't be able to control myself and the scream would just happen, then just as carefully, dragged in a fresh lung-full. I realised I was shaking all over. I had to get out of there.

Timing my movements to the beats of their wings to mask any sound, I crawled slowly back along the row of seats and under the velvet curtain. Once I was safely out of their sight, I stood up and tip-toed my way to the door, thanking with every step whoever had chosen the thick, soundproof carpet. Opening the door was terrifying. Outside was freedom, escape, but between me and it was an ancient door that was bound to creak just at the wrong moment and give me away. I turned the handle as slowly as I could, waiting for the ominous loud click I was certain it was going to make. But it didn't. The door began to swing open, the alleyway beckoned. I pushed the door just wide enough to squeeze through then closed it slowly and carefully after me, locking it with Grant's key which I quickly stuffed into my pocket before leaning against the wall to get control of my breathing and my shaking body.

I still had to retrieve my bike from behind the rubbish skip, which meant I had to walk back down the alley towards the stage door. What if they came out? What if they found me? My heart was racing. As I walked as quietly as possible towards my bike, I hatched my escape plan. In order to find me they had to come through the stage door, I reasoned to myself. If they did that, I would hear it begin to open. At that stage, I could quickly turn around and pretend I was walking away from my bike, not to it, and I could say I had just arrived. Yeah, if I am caught, play it cool. I breathed deeply, trying to convince myself that I wasn't as scared as I felt. The alley had never seemed so long. My legs felt like jelly but finally, after an eternity of terror, I reached my bike, hauled it from its hiding place, mounted and, giving up completely on silence in favour of speed, pedalled away as fast as I could.

I raced down Gloucester Street towards Linwood Avenue, my mind racing even faster. Vampires! The cute guy hiding in my bedroom was a vampire! Tasha had been axe-murdered. Someone had cut off her head. Vampires suck blood. Not in any of the movies had I heard of one cutting off someone's head. But there was always a first time. I cycled, exhausted, into our cul-de-sac and up our driveway, leaned my bike against the garage wall and hurried round to the back of the house. The lights were off in Mum and Grant's bedroom so my absence, and Severn's presence, obviously hadn't been discovered. Heaving huge sighs of relief I let myself in the back door and tip-toed down the passage to my room, stopping with my hand on the door handle. Did I want to go in?

Severn looked normal. He was asleep, curled up into a ball, completely covered by the duvet. I wasn't sure whether this was his usual sleeping style or whether he had hidden so that if Mum came in she would think it was me and not fuss. I pulled back the duvet and stared down at him. He looked peaceful. It was the first time I had seen him without a haunted, serious expression and my heart skipped a beat. His eyelashes curled delicately over his cheeks, the corners of his mouth softened in sleep. Damn, he was cute!

Get a grip, Riley, that is not the issue. Check him out. Is he a vampire or not?

Very slowly so as not to wake him, I lifted the duvet back then, just as carefully, I lifted the edge of his t-shirt. I was right. Along the length of his spine lay what I had taken to be muscles but which were, in fact, two tight rolls of what looked like creamy leather. I couldn't resist myself. I stretched out my hand and touched one of the rolls. The reaction was instantaneous.

Severn's eye's shot open, his body twisted to face me and his hand shot out, grasping my hand in a vice-like grip. I gasped with pain. He stared at me for a few seconds as sleep turned into recognition, then slowly let me go. His previous innocent expression had vanished, replaced by a look of sheer hatred.

"I know your secret," I whispered desperately. "I saw them fly."

Severn sank back onto the bed, the hatred changing to defeat.

"What did you see?" he asked quietly

I took off my jacket, dumped it in the corner and settled myself on the edge of the bed facing him.

"They were at the theatre," I began.

"Did they see you?"

"No. I was leaving when they arrived and I managed to hide. I was going to catch the Reverend and pass on your message but I didn't get a chance. When I saw them take off their shirts and fly I just freaked and ran."

"Who did you see?"

"Seth was there, but he stayed on the ground. It was the Reverend and Aiden who were flying."

"How do you know they weren't on wires?" Severn was grasping at straws.

"Huh! Yeah right! And those wings are fake. So how are they strapped on then? Come on! You've got them too, you know I've seen them. Time to tell all. Talk, Mr Jura, cut the bullshit and give me some real answers!"

Severn sat quietly, his head down, for several seconds before replying.

"Ok. What does it matter now? You've seen us so you know, but you can't tell anyone because who's going to believe you? So you may as well hear it all. Yes, there really are vampires and yes, we really are some of them. We're vampires, all of us, that's why we stick together even though, as you have probably noticed, we don't necessarily like each other. It's not like we've got a lot of other options."

"Surely there are. Why can't you just get a normal job and live in a normal house. Who's going to know? You don't look any different, well, apart from the wings. I mean, it's not like you wear cloaks and have pointy fangs."

He looked at me as if I was stupid.

"Normal! Yes, for a few months, even a few years, we may look normal." he paused as if thinking how to explain, then continued, "How old do you think I am?"

I shrugged. "Eighteen, nineteen?"

"Exactly my point," he laughed. "I've looked eighteen, nineteen, for one hundred and eleven years. I'm one hundred and twenty nine."

"Oh." I began to see his point.

"For a while, we can stay in one place, but for no more than five years at a time or people start to notice that we don't get any older and it's harder for David and myself because we look young. At least Seth and the others look like adults! David's been seventeen for over six hundred years now! No, believe me, we discovered a long time ago that the only safe thing to do is to keep moving, especially when the girls have been hunting." He added the last bit almost under his breath but I caught it.

"Hunting? You mean killing people? Drinking their blood like vampires do in the movies?"

He nodded.

"That's what you were doing the other night, wasn't it?" The image of the scene in the alley swam before me. "Did you kill that guy?"

"What?" Severn looked genuinely puzzled.

"By the nightclub, on Monday." I told him what I had seen.

"Yes." He admitted when I had finished. "But I didn't kill him. I don't kill, that's why I hunt."

"That doesn't make sense."

"Doesn't it? Figure it out! We need to keep moving but we can't afford to leave a trail of dead bodies behind us. How long to you reckon it would take before the cops started to get suspicious? The way I hunt we get what we need and nobody gets hurt, well, not seriously anyway."

"Not seriously? What does that mean? Just a few days in intensive care?"

"No, just a bit dizzy and very hungover, which they think explains why they feel dizzy. I meant it, nothing serious."

I realised that Severn was genuinely worried that I didn't believe him. A nice vampire? Nah! I was about to tell myself that nice vampires didn't exist, then I realised how stupid an assumption that would be. Most people would tell you all vampires don't exist, nice or nasty, but I was sitting on my bed talking to one, fancying him actually, so maybe I should stop making assumptions and listen.

"I go to bars and nightclubs," Severn was explaining. "The targets are easy to pick. There's always someone sitting on their own. I watch and if they're still on their own after half an hour or so I move in. Buy them a drink, talk about them, find out if they are really alone or not, if they are buy them more drinks then, when they are too drunk to notice too much, take them back to the others. The next morning they'll wake up in a park or a gutter with a hell of a hangover and some vague memories of a kinky party."

"But..." I couldn't quite formulate the question.

"They're okay," Severn reiterated. "Humans have nearly five litres of blood in their bodies, even if we all drink, we don't take more than one. Sure they'll feel rotten for a few days. Most of them will go to a doctor who will give them iron tablets and tell them to lay off the alcohol. It's not a problem."

"Unless there's a body," I quizzed. "Like the one at New Brighton the other day? Or one in Dunedin forty years ago? You killed that one, didn't you?"

"No!" Severn was adamant. "The girls did. But Seth will kill me because of it."

CHAPTER SEVENTEEN

None of it was making any sense. It was four in the morning and I was sharing my bedroom with a guy with wings who was lecturing me on the safe ways to hunt humans and suck out their blood. It was all too weird.

"Enough!" I held up my hands to stop him talking. "I don't want to know any more. At least, not right now. Let's just get some sleep. I'm going to get into my bed and you can hang by your toes from the wardrobe rail or whatever you vampires do. We just have to make sure that Mum doesn't find you."

The solution turned out to be remarkable easy. There was always a huge pile of spare blankets, discarded clothes and other junk in the corner of my room and Mum had given up nagging me about it so it was easy to hide Severn under the pile. To anyone looking in from the door he'd never be noticed, which was just as well as I had forgotten to reset my alarm and only woke up when Mum stuck her head in the door and called loudly. I made a half-hearted attempt at getting up but it didn't take much acting to convince Mum that I should stay home another day. After all, she told Grant, it was Friday, I did look very pale and we did all have to face the trauma of going back into the theatre that night. Mum and Grant had both decided to go to work as normal, which was exactly what I was hoping they would do. Now I had a whole day free to sort out a vampire.

Severn came out of hiding as soon as Mum and Grant drove away.

"It's safe," I assured him. "I've pulled all the curtains. If Mum asks I'll tell her it was because I didn't want reporters staring in. She'll buy that."

Then I found him a towel and told him that I would throw his clothes in the washing machine while he took a shower. If vampires take showers.

"Can you get your wings wet?"

He snorted.

"How do you wash them?" I had a mental picture of birds flapping their wings in dirt baths and wondered if vampires did the same.

He pushed his glasses back up his nose with one finger and raised one eyebrow over the top of the frames in his most cynical of expressions.

"With water," he said pedantically, snatching the towel from my hand and heading towards the bathroom.

The vampire that emerged looked most attractively human. And naked. Except for a towel draped around his waist but leaving an awful lot of leg and body enticingly exposed. As I walked towards him I could feel emotions bubbling and spilling through my body in physical waterfalls of desire. I hugged him close. His body, still damp, was hard under the towel.

"What shall we do till your clothes are ready?" I gasped.

He replied with a kiss, hard and passionate. I responded, kissing him back, my body telling me that the best thing, the only thing, the right thing to do would be to drag him into my bedroom. I don't know what I expect it to be like. From the tales of the girls at school who had done it, and from the enforced, single-sex human biology lessons taught by the ancient, unmarried sewing teacher, it had sounded messy, uncomfortable and downright boring. But then, they didn't have a sexy vampire.

But as quickly as my body had responded, my brain took over. Vampire! Possible killer! Hunts humans! Sucks their blood!

"Woah, wait," I pulled back and gasped. "Too ... too," I fumbled for the word, "too confusing,"

"Confusing?" Severn sounded just as confused as I felt.

"Yes, confusing. Damn it – you're sexy as anything and you are standing in my house wearing nothing but a towel – that doesn't cover much by the way – but I only met you a few days ago and since then I have found out that you are a vampire, with wings, and fangs, and all that nasty stuff. And there was a murder. And the police think you did it. Maybe you did. Maybe you'll bite me and I will be the next body and Mum and Grant will come home to find me dead on the floor and you and your funny mates all sucking my blood out with straws!" I was gibbering rubbish. I shut up. Severn looked at me and sighed. Then he laughed.

"Ok. We had better find something interesting to do though, because I could get distracted and then I might try to distract you and then if I succeeded and we both got distracted, sure as hell your Mum would arrive home. Has Grant got anything I can wear so that my towel doesn't drive you crazy?"

"Let's go see." I grabbed his hand and pulled him towards the laundry where we rummaged through the clean laundry that I had promised Mum I would fold. As I leaned over the laundry basket, Severn put his arms around me from behind, drew me close and, very gently, bit my neck. It felt delicious.

"You really do have sharp, pointy teeth," I complained later as we stood in the kitchen making lunch.

"Sorry," he grinned unashamedly. "Goes with the territory."

"It's okay. I can see now why those dopey women in the vampire movies let themselves get bitten – it's quite sexy really."

He laughed and handed me a plate of toast and a mug of hot coffee. He was back in his jeans and t-shirt and looked so normal I had to shake myself and concentrate.

"Umm," I began hesitantly through a mouthful of raspberry-jammed toast. "I know we didn't do anything ... before ... with the towel..." This was difficult. "But if we had, if we did, would it have been safe," I blurted it out quickly. Why did I blurt it out at all? I am such an idiot.

Severn's forehead wrinkled slightly as he tried to figure out what I was talking about. Then he realised. "Oh, safe? You mean would you get pregnant?"

"Or a nasty disease. After all, you drink blood. Can vampires get A.I.D.S.?"

Severn's reply was quiet and serious.

"It's not something I've ever had to think about actually. But, no, you'd be quite safe in all directions. Technically I'm a dead man. Well, no, I'm an undead man. Undead are not fertile. It's part of the change thing. I don't understand it but I do know that that's one of the things that changes. And because of the way our bodies use the blood we take in, we don't catch any diseases that are carried in the blood and we can't transmit them either. But don't ask me to explain it – I leave all that sort of science up to Finn and the Reverend, I would rather build computers."

"Right," I said. Then, because I couldn't think of anything else remotely intelligent to say I took another bite of toast. The red, blood-coloured jam ran down my chin.

CHAPTER EIGHTEEN

"So, explain something else," I demanded as I washed our dishes. "I thought vampires fed on blood. How come you guys eat pizza and chocolate. Pizzas with garlic – isn't that supposed to frighten you away?"

"Yeah, it does. Ever smelled the breath of someone who's eaten too much garlic? Words of wisdom spoken from experience – never drink the blood of someone who's just eaten garlic. But, garlic on pizzas, not a problem."

"But, but but..." I flapped my hands in the air. "You guys break all the rules. Vampires sleep in coffins during the day, turn into bats at night, are allergic to garlic and crucifixes and frizzle into piles of soot in the sunlight. Don't they?"

"Not quite. We prefer it in the dark. It's easier to hunt at night, less chance of being caught. And as we've got vastly enhanced sight and hearing, and speed for that matter, we can stay undetected under cover of darkness. And it follows – if we work at night, we sleep during the day. That's why being theatre crew is a great job for us. It's mostly night work and it's always in the dark. Black clothes, dark theatres, invisible people. Vampire paradise. Oh, and crucifixes only frighten good Catholics and I was never one of those."

"Riiight," I drawled, chewing mindlessly on my thumbnail as questions formed themselves in my brain and sorted themselves into a vaguely coherent order. "You said before that you were a dead man. Then you changed that to undead. So what's the difference, which one are you and if you're either dead or undead, how can Seth kill you so why are you hiding from him? And if your eyesight's so good, why do you wear glasses?"

"Woah!" Severn grinned. "Slow down! One thing at a time! Okay. Dead was a bad choice of word. I only said that to watch your reaction. Undead? Well, that's the opposite of dead, isn't it? Anyone who's alive is undead. Yes, we are alive. Very much so. That's the whole point. We stay that way. Forever. Or until something nasty happens and someone rams a wooden stake through us."

"Does that really work?"

"Oh, yes. So does ripping us limb from limb or any other sort of gruesome physical death. We're only human after all. We just don't die from disease or age-related thing."

"Just nasty, icky, painful things?"

"Indeed!"

"And that's what you're afraid Seth will do to you?"

"Yes."

"Why?"

"That dead guy in Dunedin forty years ago."

"Huh? I thought you said you didn't kill him?"

"And I don't know how you even know about him." He put up a hand to stop me interrupting. "I made a mistake. A serious one that Seth is never, ever, going to forgive me for. That guy was pretty weird. I had picked him up in a bar, as normal, and he was pretty drunk, but he must have had a really fast metabolism because he sobered up half way through, ah, supper. When we realised he had figured us out, Seth was all for killing him then but he was so obviously enjoying himself, I talked Seth into keeping him. He was quite happy to be a feeding snack, for the girls in particular, and I thought I could change him into one of us. It would have been the final part of the change for me and I think that's why the girls ruined it. They'll do whatever it takes to stop me flying. I'm much more fun to them as a flightless fledgling."

"What?" I was lost.

"They get it all wrong on the movies. You don't become a vampire when a vampire bites you. You become a vampire when you drink the vampire's blood. You have to bite him. That starts the process of turning you into a vampire. It also finishes the process for him. I am pretty sure that it's not really a physical change – just a really well implanted hypnotic suggestion, but until I change my first person, until they drink my blood, I can't fly. I absolutely cannot, no matter how hard I try, unfurl these stupid wings. So that was my big chance. We had found someone who actually wanted to be one of us, he was quite willing, but the girls killed him. Not because they didn't like him, but because they really don't want me to get up to their level."

"Why not? What's the big deal?"

"They are just bitches. There's no real reason except that once I can fly there is no one at the bottom of the heap for them to kick around. They like having someone to pick on. Aiden stood up to them years ago so now it's me. Like I said, they're just bitches."

"Like Tasha." I replied.

"Yes, very like Tasha. Maybe that's why I disliked her instantly."

"But if the girls killed him, the guy in Dunedin, why should you be in trouble for it?"

"Because he had handed me his business card and asked me to write our address on it so he could go home and get some clean clothes then come back to us. And I did. That was my big crime. I wrote our address on his stupid card, which the police found in his pocket. With my fingerprints on it. So now the police have a permanent record of me, which will show up every time anything happens. Like now! Seth was furious. Said I had put the whole group at risk – it didn't seem to matter that it was the girls who murdered the guy! I was the one who could be traced. And he said that if anything ever happened to put us at risk again, he would personally make sure I was no threat. He would kill me himself. And I believe him. So I'm hiding, Because I know full well that by now the police will have my fingerprints off the sound board and it won't be long before the old records turn up."

"They already have." I repeated what I had heard in the police station. Severn moaned.

"Which means we are running out of time," I continued. "Let's get thinking. Obviously the only way to get the cops off your back is to figure out who really beheaded Tasha and convince the cops we're right. Maybe that'll work with Seth as well."

Severn looked dubious. "Maybe the first part will work," he agreed reluctantly, "but Seth? I doubt it! Not to mention that the cops will want me for that body at New Brighton."

"Don't be so bloody pessimistic!" I snapped. "Have you got any better ideas? So far your only good idea has been to hide in my room! Brilliant planning!"

"Ok, okay. I bow to your superior planning capabilities. What do you suggest?"

"Well, let's start by making a list of all the things we know so far." I grabbed Mum's shopping list and pen from the bench. "So, what do we know? Timing. We know she was dead on Wednesday, before the show because she wasn't there. No, before school, because she wasn't at school."

"What about Tuesday – was she at school on Tuesday?"

"Yes."

"So it had to be Tuesday night?"

"Or Wednesday morning."

"Tuesday night's more logical. There would be cleaners and front of house people there during the day."

"So why didn't they find her?"

"Because the curtain was down. They wouldn't have gone up onto the stage."

"True. So we agree on Tuesday night."

"Right. What else do we know." Severn sauntered to the bench and began making us more coffee.

"We know she sneaked back into the theatre through the fire escape in the dressing room."

"But we don't know why." Severn handed me a mug.

"Maybe we do," I replied enigmatically. "Hang on a minute." I dashed to my room and returned to dump a crumpled ball of paper on the table.

CHAPTER NINETEEN

"It's not a lot of help," Severn said as I spread the paper out on the table. Mind you, I could have replied that he wasn't a lot of help at that moment either as his body, closely held against mine, was definitely drawing my attention away from the note. I tried to ignore the soft breath on my ear as I replied, as businesslike as possible.

"It proves she went there to meet someone."

"True, but it doesn't tell us who."

"That would be too easy, but my bet is on Jason Broderick."

"Why?"

"She wasn't wearing any knickers. She didn't go there to meet her grandmother."

Severn sniggered.

"No knickers means it was a man," I continued. "It also had to be someone she couldn't meet at any normal place or time, so that rules out the local guys."

"Unless he was married," Severn interjected.

I shook my head. "Still rules out the locals. All the married ones are about a hundred and fifty years old."

"Gosh!" Severn replied with mock horror. "Even older than me."

"Yeah, but they look it," I giggled. "Any way, you know what I mean. The only possible suspects are young (at least young-looking) and foreign. That narrows it down to you lot – Seth, Aiden, Reverend, yourself – and Jason Broderick. Off the top of my head I can rule out the Reverend – he's too short for Tasha's taste, and Aiden – because Tasha hadn't even noticed him or she would have said something. We know she fancied you but I'm going to rule you out even though you are currently the police's prime suspect, just because you said you didn't do it, you haven't axe-murdered me yet, and it is quite shocking enough that I've slept with a vampire, I don't want to think I slept with a killer as well."

"That leaves Seth and Jason." Severn had kept up.

"What about Seth? Do you fancy him as the killer"

"As A killer, yes. As THE killer, no. Not if it was Tuesday night. He has an alibi. We were all together. All night."

"So, like I said, we're left with Jason. Elementary, as

Sherlock Holmes would say."

Severn unwrapped himself from around me and sat down, peering at the note but carefully avoiding touching it. "Backstage, midnight," he read aloud.

I leaned on the back of his chair and picked the note up, turning it over on my hand to read the printing on the back.

"It's a piece off a rehearsal schedule, so it's definitely someone in the cast," I exclaimed. What I didn't add was that there was something familiar about the two words that I couldn't quite place.

"How do we prove it?" Severn pondered.

We sat, silently thinking.

"I guess I should give the note to the police," I said finally.

"With your fingerprints all over it!" Severn's tone was icy. "Good idea."

"Oops!" I felt suitably chastened for not thinking about that.

"Anyway," he continued, still dripping sarcasm, "How did you plan to explain how you got it? How did you get it?" he finished, his tone changing icy to intrigued.

"It was in her bra."

He raised one eyebrow. I laughed.

"It's her favourite hiding place," I explained. "That cleavage of hers was not all natural, it had a lot of help from underwiring and padding. All the bras in those red costumes have little pockets in them that hold the extra padding. At school Tasha would always stuff little things like money into her bra and I saw her stuff her hanky into her red costume several times. So I looked and I found! Simple!"

"Amazing!" Severn shook his head in disbelief. "But you still can't go to the police. They are going to want to know how you got into the theatre and you can hardly tell them you broke in with a master key, can you?"

"Tomorrow," I had an idea. "We've got a show again tonight. I can pretend to find it tonight and give it to them tomorrow! My fingerprints won't matter because I'll do a big excited act and they'll just think I'm stupid not to have thought about handling it carefully."

"That might just work," Severn nodded. He stood up and pulled me to him. "Any ideas how to fill in this afternoon?"

"Maybe," I replied and tilted my head back to kiss him.

It was well into the afternoon when the phone rang. I had

almost finished tidying up all references to my illicit guest and the jangling ring made me jump with guilt. I grabbed for the receiver, half expecting to hear my mother's voice say "I know what you've been doing," and sank onto my bed in relief when I recognised Anita's cheerful "Hi there".

"Hi yourself," I hoped I didn't sound as flushed as I felt.

"Are you busy?" Anita asked. "It's just that I think we should get together. I need your help. I collected all Tasha's things from her locker to take over to her mother but I think we should go through them first because I think there is a lot of stuff she might not have wanted her mother to see. If you know what I mean."

I knew exactly what she meant. Tasha's diary sprang to mind, as did her little black book with all the guys' names and dates, and scores, beside them. Tasha's mum thinks she was a sweet little goody girl. Yeah, Anita was right, maybe we should let her go on thinking that.

"Ok, but it will have to be tomorrow," I replied. "The show opens again tonight and I have heaps to do before then. How about I come to your place about eleven, then I can go straight to the theatre for the matinee."

"Ok, see you tomorrow." Anita hung up.

Well, that should be interesting. All Tasha's secret love life. I hummed a tune from the show as I waltzed through to the kitchen. Maybe I would be a dutiful daughter and start preparing dinner. Besides, I was hungry!

Severn looked up from the table where he sat reading the newspaper. With an automatic gesture, he readjusted his glasses, which made me remember.

"You never did answer my question earlier," I began as he looked at me quizzically. "If your vampire eyesight is so excellent, why do you and the Reverend wear glasses?"

He laughed. "My night vision is fantastic – it's like infra-red. My peripheral vision is fantastic. My distance vision is fantastic. I can hunt in the dark like an owl. But up close I can't see a damn thing! It's another of those weird things – everything for hunting is heightened but most physical things that were wrong with you before you change stay the same. In my case there's something wrong with the short-distance focus that vampirising didn't fix. So I can sit at the back of the theatre and see a mouse run across the back of the stage but I can't read the script on the desk in front of me." He shrugged. "David's glasses, on the other hand, are fake.

He thinks it adds to his style."

"Speaking of David," I laughed, picking up on Severn's use of the Reverend's real name, "I'll see him tonight. Should I tell him you're here?"

"Yes. No." Severn dithered. "Seth will be expecting me to contact David. They'll have someone close enough to hear everything that's said to him. And just remember, with our hearing the other side of the stage is close enough."

I suddenly remembered the strange conversation about my maglight and realised he was right. Maybe I could slip him a note if I did it carefully.

As it happened, it was Finn who slipped a note to me.

CHAPTER TWENTY

By the time Mum and Grant had arrived home, Severn and I had created a reasonable hiding place for him in the back of my wardrobe. It wouldn't be comfortable, but there was only an hour and a half between them arriving home and all of us leaving for the theatre, so we figured he could manage. After that, as long as the curtains were shut, he could wander around the house till we got home. I don't know if Mum noticed that I was being unusually helpful, but she did say that I seemed to be a lot "perkier" than I had been in the morning and that a day off school had obviously been exactly what I needed. They even agreed with my suggestion that Grant, as the society's president, should be at the theatre early in case anyone had "issues to discuss", so as soon as the television news had moved into the sports segment we were out the door and off to the theatre. I looked back as we headed down the drive and I was sure I saw the curtain in my room flutter briefly. See you later.

As it was, Grant was glad we had arrived early as stress levels backstage were intense and fights and squabbles were breaking out everywhere. Grant was soon embroiled in a deep discussion with the theatre manager about some floral tribute to Tasha they were erecting in the foyer while Mum was dragged into the wardrobe department to gossip. Setting up the stage was impossible as Dilly Davenport was drilling the dancers, moving them into new line-ups to cover the hole left by the missing Tasha, so I drifted to the back of the scenery dock where I could listen in on the conversation the stage manager was having with Seth Borman, Finn and the Reverend. They didn't look like vampires.

"I don't care whether he's guilty, not guilty or Jack the Ripper," the stage manager was saying. "I just want to know, if he isn't going to be here, who's running the sound desk?"

Surprisingly, it wasn't Seth, their supposed leader, who answered.

"I am," replied the Reverend decisively, tossing his ponytail back as he tilted his head upwards to address the stage manager who towered over his tiny figure. "Aiden's taking my place on the followspot and the girls will cover his set moves."

The stage manager beamed happily, patting the Reverend on the top of his head as if he had been a good puppy. The show would go on. Then she spotted me.

"Riley," she cried, beckoning me over. "You can help too. Aiden, go over all your set moves with the girls and divide them up. Girls, add them to your sheets. Write them down! Make sure you all know what you are doing and cover each other. We don't want any missed moves. If you simply can't do something, find a props person or even an actor to help. But," she waggled her finger as a warning," if you use an actor to move set, remind them or they'll forget!" She turned away towards the dressing rooms, her black-clad form sweeping through a bunch of milling actors like an icebreaker through the arctic sea. Scary woman! But not as scary as the creepy pair who were standing like bookends, arms folded, heads to opposite sides, staring at me from behind lashings of black mascara.

"Here," Meredith thrust a piece of paper covered in thin, spidery writing into my hand. "Pot plant, prompt side chair, piano stool, brown table, hat stand," she intoned. Maybe they looked like vampires. They did have long, black-painted fingernails and black lipstick.

"We worked it all out before," explained Aiden. "Meredith and Olivia are covering my moves, we just need you to do what you normally do plus those moves of theirs. Then they can double up on the heavier stuff."

"Ok," I shrugged. "Whatever."

Aiden was definitely too normal looking to be a vampire. Perhaps they weren't. Perhaps Severn was spinning me a line. Perhaps I watched too much television. Perhaps I never saw them fly. I caught sight of the faint wing-line under Aiden's black T-shirt. Yes he did fly! Vampires! Backstage! What would Grant think?

I stuffed the list into my pocket and walked away grinning to myself. As I did so I felt another bit of paper at the bottom of my pocket and realised I had a more important mission to achieve – finding the note I had found the other night. How was I going to make that look realistic? I stopped to stare at the dancers now huddled at the back of the stage and had an idea. Knowing they were all safely on stage and out of the way I walked purposefully to their dressing room. Sure enough, Tasha's red costume was hanging all alone on the rack. I took it down, picked up her red shoes and the box containing her headdress and, still trying to look as if I was supposed to be doing this, carried them to the wardrobe room.

"Tasha's costume," I announced as I walked in, thrusting the pile of red material forwards as I moved. "I thought it was better not to leave it in the dressing room."

"Good thinking!" the wardrobe mistress exclaimed, jumping to her feet and taking the box and shoes from the top of the pile.

I held onto the costume, walking towards the corner rack as if I was intending to hang it up. The wardrobe ladies were fussing over the headdress, so it was easy to put my hand into the bra cup and remove the hanky that was really in there while concealing the note I had hidden in my hand. But my plan was spoilt. Just as I was beginning my "Look what I found" speech, the five-minute call sounded over the intercom and the ladies began to fluster about like chickens, grabbing up bits of costume and all talking at once. Stuffing the note back in my pocket, I walked out. Plan B, show it to Grant later, tell him my prepared story of where I found it and let him take it to the police.

Once we were into the show, I was too busy with all the extra moves to think of much. I did notice that Jason looked tired and drawn. He seemed to be purposefully avoiding Dilys Davenport, looking over his shoulder to see who was near him, but he still put up a good show on stage. In fact, it was his best performance yet, which in turn spurred on everyone else. The audience applauded wildly. Grant was beaming.

I was stacking away a fake wall when Finn ambled up behind me.

"I think you dropped this," he said in his quiet drawl. He took my hand in one of his, placed something into it and folded his other hand over mine, closing my fist over the object. I was about to say that I hadn't dropped anything when he winked. Then, with a slight nod of his head, he let go of my hand and ambled away.

I opened my hand to find a large hairclip that was certainly not mine. I realised immediately that Finn was being as careful as Severn had warned me to be, as slipped inside the clip was a small square of folded paper. Popping the whole lot into my pocket as if the clip was a long-lost treasure, I slipped off to the toilets to find some privacy where I could see what was on the paper. Unfolding it carefully I read, in beautifully scripted black ink:

If Severn is safe with you, please walk past me and say, "Thank you for finding my hairclip". Then, please tell him not to panic, David and I are finding a solution.

Should I answer him? What if Finn and David were the

killers? What if they had hacked up Tasha and dropped her head in the rain truck? Hadn't Severn said David knew she was there? What if they wanted to kill Severn too? What if the note was just to get me to tell them where he was? But what if they were the good guys? What if they really were trying to help? If I pretended not to know where Severn was I might ruin his chances of getting help. They were the only friends Severn had. Severn obviously trusted them. What should I do? Decision time!

"Thanks for finding my hairclip," I said cheerfully as I wandered past Finn on my way to the scenery dock.

"My pleasure," he smiled back.

CHAPTER TWENTY ONE

Mum plonked four coffee cups down on the kitchen bench.

"Tell Severn to come down for supper," she said in a matter-of-fact tone that suggested she had known he was there all along. "Go on," she fluttered her hands to shoo me down the passage.

"How did you know?" I asked when I had returned with Severn who was now perched on the edge of a kitchen chair wringing his hands nervously.

"Ha!" Mum laughed, "Mothers know everything. You gave the game away."

"Huh?"

"You were far too cheerful, my dear. You should have been moping, worried, concerned, not happy, cheerful and oh so helpful. I figured you knew something. Plus, young man," she turned to Severn, "You crewmen must all use the same brand of after-shave. The wardrobe ladies and I have talked about it. It's very distinctive. Sort of leathery."

Severn grinned ruefully.

"Now," she said as she handed round the coffee and settled herself at the table, "what are we going to do?"

I guess we must have all been staring at her with our mouths open because she looked at us and started to laugh.

"Oh for heaven's sake!" She waved her hand at Grant. "Go get a packet of biscuits then sit down and we can all have a chat."

It all sounded so cosy!

"Really... I don't know... He could be...The police..." Grant stuttered.

"Rubbish!" Mum cut him off. "It's quite obvious Severn had nothing to do with Tasha."

"Is it?" asked Grant weakly.

"Of course it is," Mum ploughed on, ticking off her reasons on her fingers like a shopping list. "Tasha was killed on Tuesday night. If Severn was going to run away because he had killed her, he would have done it then. He wouldn't have turned up to do the Wednesday show then run. That would only, as indeed it did, make him look guilty. No, I don't know why you ran, young man, but I am willing to bet it was not because you killed that girl. Do you know something? Is that why you ran? Because you know who did it and they know you know?"

Severn shook his head but remained silent. Partly to deflect Mum from asking difficult questions and partly because I wanted to get it out of the way, I pulled the crumpled note from my pocket and laid it on the table.

"Look at this. I collected Tasha's costume from the dressing room and took it to wardrobe. I found this with her hanky in the bra padding."

Mum's hand rushed to her mouth in shock as she read the two words.

"We must give this to the police," Grant gasped.

"That's what I thought," I replied.

"I think," Mum was still on her original train of thought, "it was Seth Borman."

"What?" Severn and I both gasped.

"Well," said Mum, "think about it. She obviously went there to meet a man. They never found any knickers you know. It wasn't just that she had taken them off, she hadn't been wearing any! And she must have been up the fly tower when she fell otherwise her head wouldn't have come off."

"What?" we chorused again.

Mum looked at our shocked expressions. "Oh, apparently she wasn't beheaded. She fell or was pushed off the fly tower and on her way down she hit that flat of the New York skyline – the one made of thin sheet metal. It cut her head clean off her body." Mum looked positively gleeful as she described the gruesome image.

"Yuk!" was the best comment I could think of.

"So it might not even be murder," Grant pondered. "She may have been there all be herself and just fallen. Stupid girl playing in the theatre after dark."

"I believe that's what the police are starting to think," Mum replied. "Although I guess this note will change their minds. This," she tapped the note, "at least suggests, along with the lack of underwear of course, that she did intend to meet someone. Which brings us back to Seth Borman."

"Why Seth?" I asked. "Why not Jason Broderick? We know she was chasing him."

"The fly tower," Mum answered. "I doubt if anyone except Seth would think of going up there."

We had to admit she had a point.

"Except that Seth has an alibi for Tuesday night." Severn finally spoke. "And it's not his writing"

"Ahh," Mum's logic was defeated.

"I still think it was Jason," I interjected. "Maybe Tasha suggested the fly tower. She was into kinky sex."

Mum gasped in shock although I wasn't sure if it at the thought of Tasha's antics or my use of the word "sex". Whichever, it was an effective conversation-stopper and suddenly we were all sitting in silence, staring meaningfully into our now empty coffee cups and wishing someone else would say something. Severn broke the silence.

"Or the girls."

It was Mum's turn to say "What?"

"The girls. Meredith and Olivia. I wouldn't be surprised if it was them."

"Why do you say that?" Mum leant towards him.

Severn hesitated. "I'd rather not, um, go into details," he replied quietly. "I just think we shouldn't dismiss them as a possibility."

I could see Mum's brain go into hyperdrive. She was adding up the fact that Severn was on the run from something, her own views as to why he was running, plus what he had just said and jumping to her own conclusions.

"I thought you said you all had alibis for Tuesday night," I argued. "You said you were all together. Now you're saying you weren't?"

"Um, yes and no," Severn shifted uncomfortably in his chair. "We were all together and Seth was definitely with Finn, David and I all evening. I'm pretty sure Aiden and the girls were there all night too, but it's a big house we're renting, and there were times when they weren't always in the same room."

"Long times or short times?" I asked.

"Um, I don't know. "

"Long enough to get to the theatre and back?"

An enigmatic smile came over Severn's face. "As the crow flies, yes."

CHAPTER TWENTY TWO

I woke up at nine o'clock. Severn, who Mum had bundled off into the spare bedroom, was already up, drinking coffee and reading the morning paper. He was wearing one of Grant's red plaid working shirts unbuttoned over his crew T-shirt, a look which, with the unshaven stubble on his chin and tousled hair, was untidy but surprisingly sexy. I was glad I had decided to forego my crew blacks in favour of blue jeans, a white T-shirt and my muslin shirt, with my little bluebird still fastened around my neck and my long, blonde hair cascading loose over my shoulders. It looked good enough in my bedroom mirror. I made myself some coffee and toast and joined him, snatching part of the paper that I hoped he had finished reading.

"Your mother is amazing!" Severn said as I sat down.

"My mother is weird!" I replied. "My mother freaks me out! Her grandmother was psychic and read people's fortunes for a living. I think Mum could do the same if she wanted to. It is scary the things she knows."

"But ... her teenage daughter has a guy hidden in her room and she just... invites him for supper. It wasn't the reaction I expected."

"Me neither. But Mum never reacts the way mothers are expected to. I have a feeling you could tell her you're a vampire and she would say something like, "That's nice, dear. Don't flap your wings in the house, you'll break the ornaments"."

"Like mother, like daughter," Severn laughed. "You didn't exactly freak out either."

"I did at the theatre when I saw The Reverend and Aiden flying. I freaked out big time. It had worn off by the time I got home. By then I was just angry."

"You certainly were."

Mum passed through carrying an armful of laundry then returned immediately, heading back to collect more.

"Should we tell her then?" Severn smiled, his eyebrow shooting up quizzically.

"Ok, go for it," I bluffed. "Take your shirt off and show her your wings."

With all the perfect timing of a show music cue, noise blasted from the lounge stereo. The theme from "Lost Boys". A vampire movie! I looked at Severn, grinned and, in a bad imitation of an American accent, quoted the immortal final lines.

"One thing about living in Santa Carla I never could stomach..."

With a timing that should have taken weeks of rehearsals Mum entered the room and all three of us quoted together,

"All the damn vampires!"

We all collapsed laughing, although Mum had no idea why the two of us were so amused and, in spite of our threats, we weren't telling. She smiled as she poured herself a coffee. Maybe she knew anyway.

"What's the plan for the day?" she enquired cheerfully, settling herself at the table.

"I promised Anita I would go to her place at eleven. She's got all Tasha's stuff from school. She wants to sort through it before she takes it to Tasha's mum and I promised I would help. I figured that if I went at eleven, I could go from her place to the theatre instead of coming all the way back across the city."

"That makes sense." Mum nodded her agreement. "I want to go to the garden centre, so I'll drop you off. You can bus to the theatre."

"I'll need some money," I smiled hopefully.

Leaning back in her chair to reach the bench, Mum dragged her purse towards her, fishing out a $20 note which she handed over with the instructions to buy lunch as well and return the change. The problem of how Severn was filling in his day was solved by Grant, who emerged from his office looking grumpy.

"You're good with computers," he began, slapping his hand onto Severn's shoulder in what looked like a gesture of friendship but actually stopped Severn from escaping. "I've got a problem I'd like you to look at."

"That's him lost for the next few hours," Mum grinned. "Help me get these costumes washed and then we'll go."

With the two of us working together it didn't take long to spray stain remover on two dozen make-up covered collars and throw them all into the washing machine. Then I quickly stuffed my maglight, black jeans and t-shirt into my backpack, grabbed my jacket and joined Mum in the car where I threw my backpack into the back seat, asking Mum to bring it into the theatre later.

"He's quite mature for his age, isn't he?" Mum mused as she pulled the car out of the driveway.

"Huh?" I did a bad imitation of not understanding her.

"Severn," she smiled innocently. "He just seems a lot (she paused for dramatic effect) older (another pause to let the word sink in) than he looks."

She knows! I am convinced the woman knows! How could she? Why is my mother so normal looking but so freaky weird? I mumbled something unintelligible then quickly changed the subject to what she was going to buy at the garden centre, feigning deep interest in the colour of pansies (which I recognised) and several other fancy named plants that meant nothing at all. Still, it passed the trip to Anita's house without any further references to winged technicians.

"See you at the matinee," I called over my shoulder as I ran up to Anita's front door.

Going into Anita's bedroom is like walking through a time tunnel back into your childhood. I like Anita a lot. She's always cheerful, even when everything is going wrong – like our science experiments always do – but no-one could claim she was high in braincells. I don't think she'll ever grow out of her obsession for dolls and fluffy bunnies. Soft toys were everywhere, shelves of them lined the walls and about a hundred more jostled for space on her pink, frilly bedspread. She was even wearing bunny slippers with her jeans and a cute little pink top with diamante hearts stuck to it. But she wasn't as naïve as she looked, as proved by the smutty comments she passed as we began to read through Tasha's books.

Anita had the diary. The temptation had been too much and she had started reading it the night before, marking the best bits with pink Post-its so she could read them out loud to me. I was half listening to her while the other half of my brain was concentrating on her school exercise books. Tasha had been failing maths spectacularly. I picked up a folder, covered in a collage of film stars cut from magazines. It was labelled Theatre Arts. I flicked through the pages of photocopied notes the Dilly was so fond of handing out, searching for Tasha's project notes. We were supposed to be using the show as our practical project, so we were supposed to be keeping a journal of our thoughts and experiences. Obviously mine had left out a great deal. I wanted to read what Tasha had to say. Maybe, amongst her thoughts on the show, was a clue.

I found it. Hand-written. On the bottom of an essay. Just a

few words but as soon as I read them, thoughts started crashing into place in my head and suddenly everything made a whole heap of sense.

I must have been sitting staring at it for some time before Anita's voice finally broke through the wild thoughts whirring madly around my brain.

"Earth calling Riley! Come in Riley!"

I shook my head.

"Sorry. I was miles away." I pretended to look at my watch. "Oh, is that the time? I'll have to fly."

"What shall we do with this stuff? Her mother will have a fit!"

I thought carefully and fast. I had stopped listening to Anita's reading of the diary but there could be something useful in it. Plus I wanted that essay.

"Why don't we pack everything except the diary into a bag and you can take it to her mother. I'll take the diary and give it to the police guy — in case there's anything in there that might identify who killed her."

Anita obviously hadn't thought of that as a possibility and came over all dramatic. I sent her off to find a plastic bag and quickly stuffed the essay into my pocket while she was out of the room.

Now to go somewhere private where I could figure out what to do next.

CHAPTER TWENTY THREE

KFC won the vote as to which fast-food chain to have lunch at. I had left Anita's much earlier than I had intended and I had plenty of time to bus home and have lunch there – with Severn. But more than his company, I needed to think through what I had read on the end of that essay. Was it possible? I needed to read the last few entries in the diary. I ordered some chicken then added another piece, plus chips, potato with gravy, a pepsi (up-sized to large) and a chocolate mousse, justifying it all to myself on the grounds that it was going to be a long day with two shows and one less crew member on the floor, then carried my laden tray to a table in the emptiest part of the room.

The diary was hot stuff. It was pretty rude in parts too. I know I had told that annoying jerk at the police station that she was my friend, but the more of the diary I read, the more I thought she deserved all she got. What a cow! If she had still been alive, I would have killed her myself. I read a few of the scathing comments about me, others in our class, me and Mum and Grant, the dancers in the chorus, me and Severn, then concentrated on the last few entries.

Things had certainly heated up between Tasha and Jason Broderick. The dancers hadn't rehearsed at the same time as the actors, so she hadn't met Jason until we hit the theatre. If you took her diary as gospel she had orchestrated a pretty determined campaign to catch him. (She had planned a little side mission to trap Severn just to annoy me, and right till the last entry she thought she was winning! Silly cow!) To anyone with half a brain it was easy to see that, rather than being the handsome hero of romantic fiction, Jason was just as cheap and easy as Tasha. I doubted if she was his only conquest and I presumed he picked up a new one every show.

I read the final two entries several times as I munched my way through chips dunked in gravied potato, compared it with the note on the end of the essay and began to plan. I needed to talk to Severn.

I think better on my feet so, clutching a chicken drumstick to eat as I walked, I wandered off in the general direction of the theatre. It was only four blocks away, across the Square, but I still had nearly half an hour to kill before the theatre would be open. I detoured through the mall, wandering aimlessly through clothing shops, cd stores and strange little gift shops, oblivious to what I was looking at, thinking furiously. I arrived at the stage door just as the mechanist was opening up.

"Out front today, are we?" he asked as he turned the key in the huge old padlock and dragged open the heavy door of the leading bay.

"Huh?"

He indicated my blue jeans with a wave of his hand.

"You're not dressed to work. I thought you must be watching from out the front this afternoon."

"Oh, no. Sorry." I apologised for my lack of understanding. "I've been at a friend's place. Mum's bringing my blacks."

"They haven't caught up with him then?"

"Sorry? What?"

"Your friend. The young guy on the sound board. The one who disappeared. The police haven't caught up with him yet?"

"Look!" I tried my best exasperated tone to cover my confusion. "Yes, I was visiting a friend. But obviously not whoever you think I was with. My friend's name is A-ni-ta (I dragged it out slowly so he would get the point). She's in my class. And if you must know, we were sorting out Tasha's stuff from school to pass on to her mother!"

The last sentence shut him up. He mumbled an apology and disappeared off into the darkness of the empty theatre. I followed him inside, worrying about what he had said. If he assumed I knew where Severn was, then how long would it be before Seth and his team figured it out too. Or the police, for that matter.

How long? Not long enough. Seth before the show and the police when it finished.

The vampires arrived in a group, early as usual. What do you call a group of vampires anyway? A clutch? A horde? A swarm? In their case maybe a huddle. They walked through the scenery dock into the wings then stopped to form a tight circle. I couldn't hear anything but it looked like they were getting some sort of pep talk from Seth. Then they broke off and started their presets with such determination that I could only assume they were trying to keep busy to avoid talking to anyone outside their group. None of them looked very happy. Except the Reverend, who have me a wink and a wry grin as he passed on his way to do his pre-show checks.

It suited me fine if they didn't want to talk to any of us – I certainly didn't want to talk to them. Well, not to Seth or the girls anyway. So when I went around behind the backcloth to go to the other side of the stage, the last thing I was expecting was for Seth to be waiting for me. I know my heart missed a beat when he stepped out from beside the rain truck and clamped his hand on my shoulder.

"Where's Severn?" he growled.

Sometimes my brain reacts surprisingly fast. In a split second it registered a desire to scream, then a desire to blurt out some dumb reply like "I don't know", then it calmed down completely and I knew exactly how to deal with Seth Borman. I stopped dead in my tracks and spoke in the calmest, lowest, most determined voice I could muster.

"Take your hand off me!"

His fingers tightened their grip on my shoulder.

"Where is he?" he growled again.

"Take your hand off me," I repeated, just as determinedly. "The police are wondering what Tasha was doing on the flyfloor with no knickers on, and who she was doing it with. If you don't remove hour hand right now, I will scream very loudly, then I will say that you attacked me. Can you afford a night in the police cells, Mr Borman?"

Seth shoved me away from him and stormed off, muttering obscenities. I wanted to sit down and shake for a bit but opted instead for heading as fast as I could in the other direction, back to Mum's dressing room where I stayed until she turned up with my bag of stage blacks. By the time I had changed my clothes, most of the cast and crew had arrived and I knew Seth would be safely away in the flys dropping in cloths and flats for the opening scene.

It was a typical matinee performance – so flat I heard the stage manager asking lighting if there really were any people in the audience and, if so, were they actually alive?

The police filed in as the audience were filing out. Detective Ugly Blue Tie spotted me straight away and headed me off as I tried to make my escape. Today the tie was an explosion of orange and green – perhaps he was colourblind.

"Miss Lowe!" He stepped in front of me to block my path. "You were supposed to present yourself at the station to make an official statement!"

Present myself? I had a wicked mental picture of me, in Christmas wrapping paper with a huge pink bow, curtseying to the Queen.

"Oops, was I? Sorry."

"It is important, you know. I was hoping you would co-operate."

"Yeah, well, like I said, I didn't realise. Sorry. Anyway, I am co-operating – I've got something in my bag I was going to give to you guys."

Detective Annoying Pen Tapper didn't say anything. He just cocked his head to one side like a demented parrot and raised one eyebrow.

"I'll go and get it," I said, sidestepping him as I spoke. I dashed for the dressing rooms, returning a few minutes later to thrust Tasha's diary into his hand.

'It's her diary," I explained.

"May I ask where you got it?" he replied coldly.

"It was in her school stuff. My friend, Anita, collected Tasha's stuff from her locker to give back to her mum, but we thought you might want to see this, in case there's anything useful in it." I was trying to sound helpful; gritting my teeth and forcing myself to smile.

"Is there?"

"Pass."

"Oh come now, Miss Lowe," he wasn't even attempting to hide his disbelief, "are you telling me you haven't read it?"

"That's exactly what I'm telling you," I replied in as frosty a tone as I could manage. "I was only given it this morning – on my way here – and I have been too busy. As a matter of fact," I was getting into the swing of this untruth now, maybe I can act, "I was going to read it between the shows, but then I didn't expect you to turn up. Now you have, so you get the diary and I don't get to read it." He didn't need to know that I had already read it cover to cover, and several bits more than once. I smiled sweetly and turned to leave.

"The station, Miss Lowe! Statement! Tomorrow!" Detective Starched Underpants snapped to my retreating backside.

CHAPTER TWENTY FOUR

The cop had put me in a bad mood, so I decided to work it off. I was half way across the stage, pushing red feathers with the oversized stage broom, when I realised that he had irritated me so much about the diary, I had completely forgotten to tell him about the note. Oh well! Serves him right, poncey git!

The note got me thinking. I started making a mental list of the things I knew, ticking them off in my mind in time to my rhythmic sweeps with the broom.

One. Tasha had come back to the theatre, after it was supposedly locked up.

Two. She had got in through the fire door, which she, or someone else, had fixed for exactly that purpose.

Why?

Three. She had come here to meet someone, by invitation. They had written her a note asking her to come. No, not asking – telling! It wasn't a question, it was a command – a promise?

Why? And how did it fit with what I had read on the bottom of her theatre studies assignment?

Four. Why was easy - sex! She had come prepared. No knickers. Think! That proves there was someone else involved, and it had to be a man. If she had just come backstage to nose around or to play some kind of prank, she'd have been wearing trousers. A short skirt and no knickers definitely meant a meeting with a male.

Five. If the only person who was missing from the show, apart from Tasha, namely Severn, was not the guilty party, then the person who invited her must still be around, attending the shows and carrying on as normal. Normal? Half of them are vampires! What's normal about that?

And why in the fly tower, if it wasn't Seth Borman?

Six. Oh stuff six! Food! I stored the broom back in the wings and headed to Mum's dressing room.

"We're doing Chinese take-aways," Mum called out cheerily from behind a layer of cleansing lotion before I had barely entered the tiny room and well before I had said anything. Creepy!

"Sounds good. Where are you going for it?" I replied.

"Ah! That's the catch," Mum laughed. She rubbed her face vigorously with a paper tissue, screwed it up and threw it at the rubbish bin. "I was hoping to persuade you to go for it."

"Ah!" I replied, playing the game. I thought for a bit. "Ok. I can do with a walk. "What do you want?"

As usual in any attempt to talk me into running messages, Mum was well prepared. She simply smiled and handed me a $50 note, a list and a small jute carry bag.

"It's all on there," she smiled again.

Realising I had been truly conned into providing food for half the company, I gave in gracefully, took the bag, the list and the money, and set off out of the theatre, notes and knickerless dancers forgotten in favour of important thoughts like beef and black bean sauce or lemon chicken? Wontons or no wontons? Important stuff. Vampires were the last thing on my mind, so I jumped about a mile when one materialised beside me. I keep forgetting how quietly they move.

"Sorry," the Reverend apologised as he saw me jump.

Shoving the change from the $50 angrily into the pocket of my jeans, I spun away from the shop counter, intending to bite the Reverend's batty little head off. Then I had a better idea. Throwing my arms around him, I enveloped him a bear hug, pulling him tightly towards me in what, to the other customers in the take-away, must have looked like a reunion of long-lost lovers.

"David, sweetie, darling," I crushed him close so I could whisper in his ear, "We need to talk." Then, raising my voice back to its normal level, I dragged him to a seat in the corner and forced him to sit down. "Sugar gliders," I announced happily, knowing I wasn't making much sense, at least to the Reverend. "I used to go to the Sydney zoo all the time to watch them. You remind me of them, you know. They fly. On little tiny wings. Like little bats." I smiled knowingly. 'How's the lighting?" I appeared to rapidly change the subject, "Had any more trouble with the right-hand lavenders on the front bar?" I smiled again. The Reverend winced. He got my point. I continued to smile. "Oh, sorry, got to go, my order's ready. Gotta fly." I grabbed the containers of take-away foods, stuffed them into my carry bag and exited the shop as dramatically as I could, waving theatrically to the Reverend as if I was heading out to conquer a new land and not just trot back down Gloucester Street to the theatre.

I was back in the theatre and halfway through the scenery dock when he caught up with me.

"Fair swap," he suggested, plunging his hand into my carry

bag without waiting for my reply. "Black Forest chocolate for a couple of wontons?"

I slapped him away then conceded. "Ok, but only a couple." I opened the bag and he took one, popping it into his mouth before handing me in turn a chunk of chocolate wrapped in a piece of paper that had obviously been recently ripped off the fish and chips he was carrying in his other hand.

"Thank you, " he said around a mouthful of wonton as he wandered off.

I shoved the chocolate in my pocket and didn't think about it until much later, as I helped my mother dispose of the empty take-away containers. Idly, I fished it from my pocket and began to unwrap it. Then I noticed the writing. It was definitely fish and chip wrapper, but the writing looked like someone's idiot sheet.

"Cue forty-seven," I read. Cue forty-seven? There isn't a cue forty-seven. I had eaten most of the chocolate when it hit me. 47. Cue 4-7. Cue for Severn! I licked the remains of the melted chocolate off the inside of the paper and, sure enough, there was the rest of the message. Looking for all the world like a direction for a followspot move.

Stand by to exit. Fast travel. Stand by to pick up. Cue lampstand.

What on earth did that mean? Okay, the first bit was easy. Obviously the Reverend and Finn were organising some sort of getaway for Severn. But pick up what? Where? By a lampstand? Maybe it was just what it looked like after all. A followspot cue. At least it made sense that way. Stand by to pick up some actor who was going to be leaving the stage. Fast travel – that meant it was probably a dancer, moving fast so the followspot operator would have to swivel the big light quickly to keep up with them and keep them in the spotlight. Cue lampstand? Maybe they were to get ready when the lampstand was turned on, or off, or moved, But hang on – the Reverend wasn't on the followspot any more. He was in Severn's place on the sound board. Maybe it was something he had noticed Aiden had missed. But Aiden wouldn't miss any cues. The stage manager would be calling them to him very carefully, making sure he didn't miss any of them. And if it was for Aiden, why had the Reverend wrapped it around my chocolate? Cue 47. It had to be for Severn. Maybe he would understand the lampstand thing.

I licked the last trace of chocolate off the note and shoved it deep into my pocket. No time to think about it now. Those people who had gone home between the matinee and the evening show were starting to drift back into the theatre. Time to get back to work. Severn could explain it when I gave the note to him tonight. At the bottom of my pocket I could feel money. Money! Oh hell! I forgot to give Mum her change from the take-aways. I dashed to her dressing room and began to empty my over-stuffed pocket onto a chair, sorting the money from the rest of the junk. Maybe I should put the important note in my back pocket where I wasn't so likely to accidentally pull it out along with my maglight, or my hanky, or my idiot sheet. And what was this piece of paper? The shopping list for the take-aways. A bus ticket. Another bus ticket. So much paper!

Out of nowhere, I suddenly understood! I looked at the bits of paper strewn in front of me. All of a sudden the note made sense. The other note. Tasha's note. All of a sudden I knew why she had gone to the theatre and who she was planning to meet. Of course! It was so simple. But what could I do about it?

CHAPTER TWENTY FIVE

I don't remember much about the evening show. I went through my moves like a zombie. I presume I got the right things in the right place at the right time because nobody yelled at me, but I wasn't concentrating. I couldn't stop thinking about the notes. Both of them. I needed to talk to Severn, to make plans. In the back of my mind I also realised that "Stand by to exit. Fast travel." meant Severn would soon be leaving, and I didn't want to think about that.

All I wanted to do when the show finished was go home, but that wasn't going to happen. Even though Tasha's death had squashed the plans for the mid-season cast and crew party, Grant and the committee had decided that everyone needed some sort of bonding exercise to try and keep things as normal as possible, so a quiet supper was being held back at the society's rehearsal rooms. I knew Mum secretly wanted to go home as much as I did, but we had to do our bit and support Grant. Mum agreed we could probably sneak away after an hour or so and Grant nodded, adding that he thought the whole thing was only a token gesture and would wind itself up pretty quickly.

He was right. It was flat. Quite the opposite to the riotous affair at our place a week earlier. No Dilly and Tasha, the duelling dancers. Everyone stood or sat around in quiet huddles, sipping more fruit juice than wine and nibbling on delicate club sandwiches of indeterminate and mysterious-looking fillings. The note seemed to be burning a hole in my pocket. I was sure the vampires could sense its presence. I was getting paranoid. For the short time they were there, they ignored me. The junior horde sat quietly together at a corner table while Seth targeted the few people he needed to speak to, Grant being one of them, then he beckoned them with a sweep of his arm and they all obediently trotted after him. Off to hunt, no doubt. I rushed over to Grant.

"What did he want to talk to you about?" I demanded.

"Don't panic." Mum hung coyly on Grant's arm. "It wasn't..." she waved her arms expressively trying to say in a gesture that he hadn't mentioned Severn. "He was just being polite. Waving the flag and apologising for not staying. Not that we expected them to. It's not exactly an exciting evening's entertainment."

I relaxed.

"No, it's not. Can we go soon, please?"

Grant looked at his watch.

"Another fifteen minutes?" he asked, hopefulness giving him that spaniel puppy expression he does so well.

"Ok," I sighed. "Another fifteen minutes. Then I'm dragging you out by the hair."

I wandered aimlessly back to the food table and was debating having another slice of cake, so I didn't notice Finn and the Reverend come back in.

"Where can we talk, privately?"

For the second time today he made me jump. With just a slight nod of my head to tell them to follow me, I turned and left the room. The rehearsal rooms were above a row of shops. Above them again were offices. I headed up the stairs and sat down on the top one. They sank down to join me.

"Sugar gliders." the Reverend began.

"Where's Seth?" I was still paranoid.

"Nightclubbing. Don't worry; we don't want him here either. But we don't have long or he'll notice we're not there. Now... sugar gliders?"

I giggled. Then I came straight to the point.

"I know your secret. I saw you and Aiden fly. At the theatre. Hanging the lights."

"You told Severn?"

"Yep."

"And he's okay with this?"

"Yep."

Finn and the Reverend looked at each other and seemed to come to a mutual decision. The Reverend continued.

"Well, I guess that makes the next step a whole lot easier. One less set of lies and deceptions we have to deal with. I take it Severn is with you?"

"Yep again."

"Your parents are in on this too?"

"Yep again."

"Do they know as well?" Finn broke in, in a tone of total disbelief.

"Nope. Not about the wings. Well, Grant definitely doesn't know but Mum is one of those weird psychic witchy women and she may know, but it's impossible to tell with her. But we didn't tell her."

Finn buried his head in his hands, sighing deeply. The Reverend just closed his eyes and shook his head in bewilderment before continuing.

"Ok. So he's safe for now. But it is a bit obvious. I would imagine it shouldn't take long for either Seth or the police, or both, to figure it out and the police, at least, can simply bring a warrant and drag him out. So we have to act quickly. I guess you read the note, but I also suppose it is irrelevant now as we can just tell you and you can tell Severn. Transport is on its way. I will have his new passport and papers by tomorrow." He checked his watch. "We can't stay, Seth will be getting twitchy. But we need to talk to Severn. It's your city – where's a good place to meet?"

I thought quickly.

"My school. Eastgate High. It's on the main road by the mall. There's a statue out the front, with a stone wall behind it. We could meet there."

"Ok," he checked his watch again. "Give me a couple of hours."

"Ok," I sighed in agreement. Yet another night without sleep.

CHAPTER TWENTY SIX

"Why didn't you just tell them to come to our place?" Mum asked the obvious question.

We were back home, sitting around the dining table, nursing cups of drinking chocolate, in what was fast becoming a regular habit. Severn was studying the obscure, slightly chocolate flavoured note from the Reverend, and I had just finished explaining some, if not all, of my conversation.

"Because I didn't think of it," I answered honestly.

"Hmm," Mum was thinking. "Severn, I presume you can drive?"

Severn nodded.

"Then take the car. It will save a lot of time, you won't get so cold and, if there are any police cruising around the neighbourhood, you won't be so noticeable." She pulled the car keys from her pocket and slid them across the table to Severn who mumbled his thanks, his mind still puzzling the note.

"I don't get the lampstand bit either." He gave up and pushed the note away.

"Well," said Mum, draining the last of her drink, "Grant, move yourself. Let's leave them to puzzle it out and get some sleep. Be careful you two," she added as they left the room.

I waited till I was sure they were out of earshot.

"They know that I know about the wings."

"How did they take it?"

"Surprisingly well. Almost relieved. The Reverend said it made it easier - one less set of lies to tell. Come on, let's go now. They might get there early."

"Where do you think you will be going?" I asked as we drove out of our street and turned towards Linwood Avenue.

"I don't know," Severn shrugged a reply as he concentrated on figuring out the workings of Mum's car.

"Maybe there are other groups of you and you'll be sent to one of them," I guessed. "What do you call a group of vampires anyway? A horde? A tribe? A coven?"

"I don't know. A roost? A swarm?" Severn laughed. "I don't know if there is a term specifically. Is there a term for a group of teenage girls?"

I got his point.

"Seth calls us a guild," Severn continued, swinging the car around the traffic island to bring it to a halt outside the school gates.

We didn't have to wait long before the black-coated figures of the Reverend and Finn appeared walking around the corner from the side street. Severn gave one quick blast on the car's horn and they hurried over to climb into the back seat. Severn reached over the seat to shake hands with both of them.

"Hi guys, thanks for coming to help."

"Are you all right?" Finn was genuinely concerned. Severn nodded.

"Right!" The Reverend clapped his hands together to get our collective attention. "We have a lot of things to say and not long enough to say it all, so let's get started. The best thing we can do for you right at this moment is get you out the country and out of Seth's way. Once you're safe, I will deal with Seth."

"You will deal with Seth?" Severn sounded incredulous. ""Do tell me how?"

The Reverend smiled sweetly and rubbed his hands in glee.

"Let me tell you a story."

"There isn't time for stories," I butted in. "You just said so! How are you going to get him away from here and where are you sending him? Are there more ... colonies? ... is that the word?... of you lot?"

"Severn? Finn? Do you want to answer that?" the Reverend looked from one to the other.

"I thought there was just us," Severn shrugged. "Otherwise I would have been out of here long ago."

"That's what Seth wants you to think," the Reverend replied. "That's how he keeps his power over you. But it isn't true. Now, can I tell you a story?"

"We're not a huge group," he continued, " and we may not be the only ones. We don't know if there are any others because we don't exactly advertise and neither do they, but logic suggests there could be other groups out there somewhere. If there are, with the help of the internet, we can probably begin to make contact. However, for now there is just the Order as we know it. About fifty of us. We live in a monastery, on a mountain, in the south of France. I own it."

All our mouths dropped open at once. The Reverend giggled at our surprise.

"We told you and Tasha, Riley, that I was called the Reverend because I am. Reverend Father, actually. I'm a monk. When I was a child, back in the 1340s, if you wanted a good education you joined the church, so I was packed off to the nearest monastery – which just happened to be on land owned by my father. It was a weird place, with a reputation for receiving visits from angels. The local peasants kept insisting to my father that they saw angels flying over the monastery at night. Don't you think it's much nicer to be thought of as an angel than as a vampire?

"Anyway," he continued, "the Black Plague struck and people were dropping dead all over the place. Lots of the ordinary monks died. I was saved by an angel. Okay, some of us were saved by being transformed by the Abbot. Twenty eight of us survived the plague, twelve of us still live in the monastery. Which, as I said, I now own as my father and the rest of my family did not survive the plague."

"So, if you actually run the show," I broke in, "why is Seth in charge and, come to that, why are you here at all?"

"This is where the story gets interesting." The Reverend settled back in to the car seat and made himself more comfortable. "Seth was a mistake. We make them from time to time. He joined us about three hundred years ago. He comes from a privileged background, as do a lot of us, but whereas some of us believe in equality and intelligent government by mutual agreement, Seth believes he is better than everyone and should, therefore, be the one in charge. He has never been able to get his head around the fact that we rule ourselves by a committee. His biggest ambition is to take over the committee, throw them all out and run the place himself."

"Them?" Finn interjected. "You own the place but you're not on the committee yourself?"

"No," The Reverend replied. "Because I own the place. I didn't want to have too much influence, and I prefer to keep a low profile, but I do have a casting vote if necessary."

"Seems fair," Finn nodded in approval.

"Seth was so determined he was the only one with the ability to run the Order, we decided to let him put his money where his mouth was, so to speak. The committee told him to leave the Order and travel for two hundred years, putting together a group of his own and proving he could deal with all the problems that come with not appearing to age, and needing to feed. Then he could return and his place on the committee would be voted on again. He thought that was an easy assignment. He also thought that I went with him because I was just as disgruntled with the committee as he was. He has no idea of my real position and no idea that my real job in this little escapade was to watch him, evaluate his leadership abilities and send constant reports back to the monastery. He also has no idea that he has completely failed the test."

"So where does that leave me?" Severn inquired.

"On your way back to France, as soon as the Lear jet arrives. It had to be diverted from a run to Stockholm so it should arrive about 2am Monday morning – in about 24 hours time."

"Won't the police have the airport security watching for me?"

"Indeed, but they will be watching for Severn Jura travelling on a British passport, not Brother John-Benedictine travelling on diplomatic immunity from the Holy See."

"The holy what?" I asked "And isn't Benedictine a drink?"

"The Holy See. You'll be travelling on a Vatican passport," the Reverend explained. "One of the benefits of being a monk – especially monks with printing presses and hundreds of years' experience in passport forgery." He grinned. "And yes, it's a very nice drink – invented by a monk. Now, Severn, your passport should arrive by courier tomorrow. I will get it to Riley during the show. All you have to do is get yourself to the airport by 2am and wait for the plane. Any other questions?"

"What will happen to Seth?" Finn asked quietly.

"The jet won't just be collecting Severn, it will also be dropping off Brother Martin. He and I will deal with Seth," the Reverend replied, his tone guarded.

"And us?" Finn continued.

"We will continue to crew the show for the rest of the week. The last thing we need is for our troubles to impact on others. We have signed a contract to work this show and we will honour that contract. All of us except Severn, for obvious reasons. After pack-out everyone will be taken back to the monastery where Seth, and Olivia who is positively dangerous and a very nasty woman, will answer to the charges I will be putting forwards, and they will be dealt with by the Order's decision. You and your children will be welcomed, although Meredith may need some serious counselling to undo the damage done by Olivia and Seth's influence."

"Your children? Meredith and Aiden are your children?" I was gobsmacked.

"Yes," Finn sounded tired. "Aiden watched Meredith being changed by Olivia and Seth. He told me and we both allowed ourselves to be changed to keep Meredith safe. I don't know if we succeeded." He turned to the Reverend. "If you want anyone to testify against those two, Aiden and I will be willing to speak out."

"Thank you," the Reverend replied. "I will make sure you have your chance. Now, it's getting late. Severn, can you drop us off a couple of blocks from the flat?"

"Hey," I said later as we pulled Mum's car into the garage. "I've just remembered another thing I didn't want to say in front of Mum and Grant – well not yet anyway. I know who killed Tasha. I know who wrote the note."

"What?" Severn was incredulous. "Who? Can we prove it?"

"Maybe we can." A plan was beginning to formulate in my head. "Maybe we can."

CHAPTER TWENTY SEVEN

There was now less than twenty four hours before Severn was going to be whisked away to the other side of the world, out of my life possibly forever. So it seemed a tragedy to waste any of those hours sleeping. But that's exactly what I did. In fact, I slept late and didn't wake up till after eleven o'clock in the morning. With the Sunday show scheduled for four o'clock that meant four hours maximum before we had to get to the theatre for the pre-set, then another eight hours between the show ending and Severn's flight taking off. I had slept away nearly half of our last day. Great!

I wandered bleary-eyed down to the kitchen in search of a cup of strong coffee to wake me up and met Severn in the hallway, coming out of Grant's office.

"Come here," he said, beckoning me into the office. "Come and see what I've done." He walked over to the computer and sat in front of it.

"Look," he said, tapping keys and clicking with the mouse, "I've set you up your own profile on Grant's machine. If you log off from him (he showed me on the screen the steps as he was explaining them) you can log on again as yourself. Then, if you click this icon (he demonstrated again) you can connect to the internet and check your email."

"I don't have an email account," I pointed out.

"You do now. I've set up a Hotmail account for you. As soon as I get to wherever I'm going I'll set myself up and email you. Then we can keep in touch."

"Fabulous!" I hugged him gratefully. "I'll check it every day."

"Umm, you'd better give me a week to get organised," he replied, shutting the computer down as he spoke. "I have no idea where I'm going to end up. Actually," a thought struck him, "this may be pointless. I don't even know if this monastery place has electricity, let alone internet access."

"It must have," I reasoned. "Well, electricity anyway. Or the Reverend wouldn't have been able to get help from them so quickly."

"Yeah, right!" Severn didn't sound impressed. I told him so.

"I don't know if I am," he replied. "I've been thinking. It's all very well for him to come over now as the superhero who saves the day, but why did he wait this long? I've been with this lot for one hundred and eleven years. Sure, the first twenty or so were fun, a bit exciting, a bit different, but then things, or Seth and Olivia to be precise, started to turn nasty. For the last ninety years ... ninety years! ... my life has been hell. And last night I find out that he could have done something about it. That sanctimonious, pious little religious git has sat there, for ninety years, and watched me live through all kinds of abuse. And he's done nothing to stop it. Nothing! A couple of days ago, when I thought he was just another downtrodden servant of Seth like the rest of us, I wouldn't have, I hadn't, thought anything about it. But to find out that he's got all this power and influence and he's sat there and watched, it makes me sick!"

"Yeah," I said quietly, not really knowing what to say to diffuse his increasing anger. I was thinking of school and all those days when you hated being there, and how I couldn't wait till the end of the year when it would be all over. Then I tried to imagine it going on and on and on for ninety years. It was way beyond my comprehension. "Yeah."

"It's bad enough for Seth to treat us like garbage just because he's bored, sadistic and power-crazed, but for David to have the means to stop it and not to do so, because he's playing his own little social experiment game on Seth, it's too much!"

"So what are you going to do about it?"

"I haven't decided. But I do know one thing – this is just the beginning. I took all that garbage from Seth because I genuinely thought there was nowhere else I could go. Now I know differently. I have alternatives. Other ways to live. And none of them involve taking crap from anyone. Not any more. But," his tone changed abruptly as if he had flicked a switch in his brain and turned his anger off, "I don't want to think about that at the moment. Let's talk about something pleasant, like murder and death and headless dancers. You have a plan?"

"I certainly do. Let's go to the kitchen and get coffee and food and I will explain."

We wandered down the hall and while Severn made himself useful toasting hash browns, I spread the notes out on the table and explained my theory about Tasha's killer, and my plans to prove it.

"Why bother?" Severn asked.

"Because," I answered, stalling while I swallowed a

mouthful of hash brown, "if I went to Detective Frostface with this, even if he believed me, there is absolutely no proof. They would just deny it. The police think you did it and it's much easier to blame it on an outsider. I know from school, if something goes wrong the locals will always gang up against any of us 'foreigners'. So who are they going to blame this time? One of the cast? Or one of those weird travellers who we don't know enough about to trust? Anyway, just like you want to stick one to both the Reverend and Seth, I want to stick one to that cop. He's horrible. He gets right up my nose and makes me angry and I want to prove a point."

"What point?"

"I don't know," I shoved another hash brown into the toaster, "Any point! I want to get some proof then hand him the whole parcel, all wrapped up in a big Christmas bow."

"And I thought Olivia was mad," Severn sighed in resignation. "Ok, let's go over this plan of yours again."

CHAPTER TWENTY EIGHT

By the time the show broke for interval my plan was already in action. No stopping it now. This time it was my turn to pass a note, beautifully but anonymously typed on Grant's computer and sealed in an envelope with their name typed on the front. I had waited till one of the big production numbers, when all the cast and dancers were on the stage and the crew were poised for the next quick scene change, before quickly pinning the note to the backstage noticeboard. It didn't matter if it wasn't found till the show finished, in fact, it was probably better if it wasn't. We still had six hours between the show ending and midnight, which is when the note said to meet. Would they take the bait? I didn't think I had left them much choice.

I know you killed Tasha.

What price will you pay for my silence?

Backstage, midnight tonight.

That should get their attention. It's not like I was actually going to bribe them, I just needed to make sure they came to the theatre. Okay, it was a bit over-dramatic, but I would hate to think all those theatre arts classes had been for nothing. I did need to get them backstage, not just because it was truly dramatic – scene of the crime and all that – but because I wanted to use the show's microphones to record their confession. But, let's face it, it didn't have to be midnight. Any time after the show was over would have done. That was just me being melodramatic. Too many late night horror movies.

With the note safely delivered, I rushed to the scenery dock to get my piece of stage set ready for the end of the song. Finn passed me, going the other way, towards Olivia and Meredith who were already poised with their pieces ready in the wings.

"Cue forty seven," he said quietly as he passed.

I dashed into the dock and checked my piece of set – a street lamp. Sure enough, I could see the edge of a manila envelope sticking out from under its base. I glanced as inconspicuously as possible back to Finn and noticed that he was distracting the girls' attention away from me. I reached down and retrieved the envelope and stuffed it quickly into the waistband of my jeans, feeling the shape of the passport inside it, before hastily shoving and hauling my lampstand out of the dock and into place for the move. The assistant stage manager noticed I was late and waggled a reproving finger at me. Not that it mattered. I was still in the right place at the right time, even if it was only with seconds to spare. Hopefully the envelope would stay in place till I could sneak it into my bag at interval.

I nodded my acknowledgement to Finn as I trundled the street lamp back into its place in the scenery dock as the scenes on stage changed yet again, then practically forgot about the envelope stuck down my jeans as the show sped remorselessly towards interval. The rain truck was pushed into place and the crew unconsciously, as we had done every performance since last Wednesday, held our breaths until we saw the water was, well, water coloured. Last Wednesday! Only four days ago. It seemed like a lifetime.

The number ended and I moved forwards to take my part in hauling the huge truck back to its storage place at the very back of the stage. As I did so, I almost banged into Jason, who was dripping water and drying his hair with a towel as he hurried to his dressing room to change his clothes.

"Get out of my way," he snarled rudely, pushing me as he spoke.

"Get stuffed!" I snapped back. "Bloody actors," I added under my breath as I put my shoulder against the rain truck and began to push. "He's a bit stressed tonight," I said to Beth who was beside me, helping to push.

"Yeah," she replied. "I've been watching him the last few days. It's getting to him, this Tasha thing. In some ways, I've got to hand it to him, he's done his part to keep this show together. When we restarted on Friday night, the atmosphere was terrible. It was pretty obvious that some people didn't want to be here at all. Some of us were just plain scared. I mean, let's face it, someone lured that poor girl back to the theatre and cut her head off. And it has to be one of us. It's enough to give you the creeps. Somehow on Friday Jason found the energy, the professionalism, to go out on stage and give a really good performance, and then everyone else had to do the same. And he's kept it up every show. Even if he does look like shit under the make-up. I wasn't impressed by Jason Broderick when he first arrived, but I have to admit I am now."

"Heads!" Seth's voice commanded from above and we quickly ducked out of the way as he lowered the huge backcloth back into place, concealing the rain truck from the audience once again.

"That's us done," Beth said, rubbing her hands in satisfaction. "Coffee break."

Finally, a chance to get rid of the envelope. Fortunately Mum and her friends were all away in the Green Room getting their drinks and their dressing room was empty, so it was easy to remove the envelope from my waistband and stash it at the bottom of my bag. Grabbing a can of coke, I followed them to the Green Room. I felt like some company but I didn't fancy the alleyway. Not today. Not without Severn.

However, the Green Room was too small for the huge cast and was already overflowing with people. The smell of sweaty bodies and make-up was too much for me, maybe the alleyway was a good idea after all. I quickly turned away only to crash into Jason Broderick for the second time in ten minutes.

He snorted in exasperation, raising his hands to push me aside like he had done backstage. I held my ground and, dropping my accent back to its best Australian twang, which I knew would carry over the Kiwi vowels and penetrate the hum of conversation in the Green Room, challenged him to try it.

"Go on, mate, hit me again. I dare you."

Jason stopped, his hands still raised. I carried on, moving towards him, pressing my advantage, aware that the conversation behind me had almost stopped and we were rapidly becoming the centre of attention.

"Look, mate, you were in the wrong before, not me. You came off the wrong wing. I was exactly where I was supposed to be, doing my job. Do you have a problem with that? Or do you just get some kind of thrill pushing girls around? "

Jason muttered something unintelligible, his raised hands turning into a position of surrender. He backed away. I kept coming.

"Do you do it often, mate? Do you always push around girls who don't do what you want? Bad habit, mate. You'll do it once too often."

As he cowered back against the corridor wall, I walked slowly and determinedly past him, my head held high. Shaking could wait till I found somewhere private. I headed for the ladies toilets and shut myself in a cubicle until I heard the stage manager call Act two beginners.

Once the work lights were off and the backstage area was plunged back into darkness, I felt a little more comfortable. I took up my favourite position in the wings where I could watch the action on the stage but not be in anybody's way. I didn't need another confrontation with Jason Broderick. I certainly wasn't prepared for the confrontation I did have.

Not that I objected to it when it happened. I was facing the stage, not taking much notice of what was going on around me, so I didn't hear him approach. First thing I knew, a pair of strong arms wrapped themselves around me from behind.

"Hi," Severn's voice whispered softly in my ear.

"Hi," I spun around and returned the hug. "What are you doing here? What if Seth sees you?"

"What if he does?" Severn laughed. "He will have heard me by now, any way. They all will have. Hi guys." I knew he was speaking to the other vampires, and I knew they could hear him, even though he was speaking barely above a whisper and they were stationed all over the theatre. "Yeah, it's me, Seth." He paused as if listening, which I knew he was, "No, Seth, I don't intend to see you later. I don't give a stuff what you want. Not now, not ever. Have a nice day!" Severn looked upwards to where Seth stood in the fly tower, smiled sweetly and raised two fingers in a gesture of defiance.

I giggled, but I was concerned. He seemed to be inviting retaliation.

"What are you playing at?" I hissed.

"A new way of looking at things," Severn replied seriously. "I've been thinking about all the stuff David said. And Seth simply doesn't bother me any more. It's a power and knowledge thing. Seth had the power because he had the knowledge. Now I have the knowledge as well, the power shifts. Sorry, Seth," he smiled up towards the flys, "You don't scare me any more."

I looked approvingly at the reformed Severn. The new look was more complete than I had realised. Instead of the scruffy jeans and crew T-shirt he had been wearing for the last few days, he was now clad in stylish black dress slacks and a matching black shirt that looked suspiciously like real silk.

"Wow!" I said approvingly. "Where did the clothes come from?"

"I got bored," he replied, "I went shopping."

"You what?" I was horrified. "With the police looking for

you? You went shopping?"

"Yes, I did. Come on, Riley, the last place they are going to look for me is a shopping mall. Plus they are looking for someone scruffy, unkempt and sleeping rough, not someone in business clothes. It's a great disguise. And I've had a lot of practice at not being noticed. Don't stress. Haven't you got a park bench due about now?"

"Damn!" I pulled away just as the lights on stage faded to a blackout, and hurried on stage to collect the bench. When I came back, Severn was talking quietly to Finn. I ran through to Mum's dressing room, rummaged in my bag for the envelope containing Severn's new passport, then dashed back and thrust it without explanation into his hand. As I turned away to get my next piece of set, I glanced at the noticeboard. The letter was gone. It wasn't only the show that was heading for final scene.

CHAPTER TWENTY NINE

Even though he was keeping a low profile, the news of Severn's presence spread rapidly through the gossip network, so by the time the final curtain went down and the house lights came up, people were queuing to get a piece of him. The stage manager got in first, grabbing him by the shirtsleeve as he helped me stack away a set of chairs.

"Mr Jura," she delivered him a determined, don't-mess-with-me, crocodile smile. "How kind of you to grace us with your presence." The sarcasm dripped like vinegar. "Is this a fleeting visit, or are you expecting me to welcome you back with open arms and tell you it's quite all right, I just love it when crew run out on my show with no warning. I take it that, seeing you've dared to show your face, you've already been arrested and charged and that, for some reason known only to a handful of rich lawyers, they have let you loose on bail?"

"Stop right there!" Severn put up a hand to interrupt her tirade. "I have not been arrested, nor will I be." The new, assertive Severn volleyed her anger and sarcasm straight back at her, his back straight and his speech pedantic. "I will apologise to you for missing the last few shows, however, I will also point out that I did not run out on the Wednesday show – I completed it and then I left hurriedly. My reasons were urgent – but they were also personal and I will not explain them to you. I can only offer my sincere apologies that I was then unable to advise you of my impending non-appearance."

The stage manager was dumbfounded, as was the growing crowd watching the scene. Apart from Severn's surly replies to the music director, I don't think she had ever heard him speak more than a couple of words, and those were usually mumbled and deferential. Severn rocked back on his heels, crossed his arms in front of him, cocked his head slightly to one side and delivered a disdainful, take-it-or-leave-it look that didn't need any more words to put across the clear message that Severn was not open to negotiation.

"Is this a fleeting visit?" Severn continued, repeating her words. "Unfortunately yes. I have to..."

"Severn!" Grant pushed through the crowd, grabbed Severn's arm and began to haul him away. "I need to talk to you urgently, young man." He tapped my shoulder with his spare hand and I followed them through the parting he had created in the audience, who were beginning to disperse as they realised the best part of the show was over. Once we reached the relative privacy of the scenery dock, Grant thrust his car keys into my hand.

"Get out of here now," he hissed urgently. "Someone backstage has just phoned the police to tell them you're here. Go now! I'll put them off. Wait for us at the car." Grant emphasised his words by physically pushing us towards the stage entrance. We didn't need to be told twice. Clutching the keys, I grabbed Severn's hand and we slid out the door and bolted down the alleyway.

"This way," I urged, turning left as we got to Gloucester Street. "We're in the carpark building. Hurry!"

Severn had been right, vampires can move fast. Holding his hand as tightly as I could, I was dragged along the street, my feet barely making contact with the pavement. We crossed the road at a run, against the green light, and raced into the welcoming gloom of the carpark stairs.

"Level four," I explained, puffing. "Hang on, I need to get my breath back."

"Grant's okay," was Severn's only comment as we slowly climbed the stairs and unlocked the car.

My reaction to his comment was to have one of those moments when a whole heap of images and thoughts all explode in your head in a fraction of a second. A memory of Mum and Dad in Australia, fighting as usual. A picture of Grant's spaniel smile. Grant at his computer, trying to sound like he knew what he was doing. Mum and Grant in the kitchen, singing duets. Mum smiling. Dad's letter wanting me to move back to Oz. A new baby. Grant carrying the groceries. Grant in the garden. Mum smiling.

"Yeah," I answered. "Grant's okay. You, on the other hand, are a dumb-arse! What on earth did you think you were doing, turning up at the theatre? Let me guess – you've got Seth all sussed so everything else will be sweet? Did you forget you are at the top of Detective Frogface's hit list of prime suspects?

Severn didn't even attempt to answer. He was as angry as I was. Great, I'm alone in a deserted carpark building with a gorgeous man who is about to be whisked away to the other side of the world and we sit, too angry to speak to each other.

Excellent, Riley! Brilliant move! After a few minutes of stony silence, the whole thing got to me and I started to laugh. He looked sideways at me, the tension evaporated and he began to laugh too. Then he kissed me. Not a bad way to apologise. I kissed him back. After all, we had to do something to fill in the time while we waited for Mum and Grant, who appeared, slightly flustered looking, about thirty minutes later.

"Well, that was my best acting role all season," Grant began as he settled himself into the driving seat and clipped up his seatbelt.

"What happened?" I wanted all the details.

"Oh, a couple of constables arrived clutching a warrant for your arrest, Severn. Luckily for you, and unluckily for them, it took them about fifteen minutes to get the three or four blocks from the police station to the theatre, so my explanation that you had left already seemed quite reasonable. I don't think anybody had even the slightest idea that good old Grant Watson was being anything other than the helpful society president."

"What did you tell them?" I asked.

"I just said that Severn had spoken to me briefly than left, and then I added, ever so helpfully, that he had asked what bus to take to get to Sydenham." Grant chuckled and I realised he was enjoying this immensely.

"You lied to the police? You sent them to the other side of the city?" I said incredulously. I was going to have to totally re-think my opinion of Grant, there was a lot more to him than I had realised.

"Noooo," Grant acted the innocent. "I may have been economical with the truth but I didn't lie. I'm sure Severn asked me once about buses to Sydenham. It may have been a week ago and, come to think of it, it may have been Aiden, but ..." his sentence trailed off into a shrug of his shoulders. "But," he continued, his tone changing to businesslike, "now we need to make plans. Where do we go from here?"

"If you've sent the police off on a wild goose chase, can't we just go home?" Mum asked. "I'm hungry."

Grant shook his head.

"I don't think it's the best place to take Severn right now. I have a feeling they could turn up and if they do, they'll be carrying a warrant. I think we need to find somewhere else to stash Severn for a couple of days."

"Just till later tonight, actually," said Severn. "David has arranged for me to go and stay with some, ah, friends of his. All I need to do is get to the airport by 2 o'clock in the morning."

"In that case," Grant started the car, "we'll go to my office. Don't worry," he smiled at Mum, "we won't starve, there's a takeaway just around the corner, we can grab some fish and chips. It'll be like a picnic."

CHAPTER THIRTY

Grant's choice was a good one. His company had a building on the edge of the Central Business District. The street was a mixture of commercial offices and light industrial warehouses so, early on a Sunday evening, it was deserted. Also, Grant's building had its own underground carpark, making our presence undetectable by anyone passing by. Grant punched the buttons on the security panel and slid the car into the garage when the huge metal doors opened temporarily to let us in. Another button push and they closed behind us, locking automatically. We piled out of the car and followed Grant as he led the way to his office on the seventh floor.

"Make yourselves comfortable," he invited. "Sue and I will go out and get some food. Back soon."

As they left, Severn hauled the envelope from his pocket and began to open it.

"Let's see what David has come up with," he said, pulling out the passport.

It was even more realistic than I had expected. I mean, I knew it was going to be good – it had to fool Customs, but I somehow expected it to be new. Instead, it was suitably worn, as if it had been well used, and inside were lots of different customs stamps. Brother John-Benedictine was well travelled.

"That makes sense," I said, pointing out the stamps. "If you work for the Vatican, and you're leaving New Zealand, you must have arrived here in order to leave again." It made sense to me.

Severn nodded. "Yeah, right."

I recognised the passport photo from the sullen expression on Severn's face.

"That's cut out and blown up from the cast and crew photo," I laughed. You looked so grumpy."

"I was. If you remember the photo that well, you will remember I was standing next to Tasha. She had her hand on my buttocks!"

'What? Like this?" I grabbed his bum playfully.

"No," he replied in kind. "More like this."

We were still deciding this issue when Mum and Grant returned with the food, although by the time they had covered the distance from the lift to the office, we were sitting innocently,

Severn reading a computer magazine that was lying on Grant's desk and me swivelling happily in his big executive chair. I don't think Mum was fooled at all.

We spread the fish and chips out on Grant's desk.

"What's next?" Mum asked around a mouthful of fish.

Grant chewed thoughtfully on a chip before answering.

"I think we, you and I," he indicated to Mum and himself, "should go home for a few hours and act normally. Just in case the police do decide to turn up there. We can say we haven't seen Severn since he left the theatre. Worst they can do is search the place and he won't be there. These two," he indicated Severn and myself, "can stay here and keep each other company for a while. Then we can come back in a few hours, pick them up and deliver Severn to the airport."

Mum nodded her head in agreement.

"I have a feeling that, as responsible parents, we shouldn't be leaving our poor, defenceless little girl alone in the dark with a strange male, but I have a sneaking suspicion she can cope."

"Yeah but can I?" asked Severn "Will I be safe?"

I threw a chip at him.

"Obviously not," Mum replied. "Come on Grant, let's go."

I stopped them just as they were about to leave.

"Grant?" I tried to sound innocent. "I don't suppose you could let me have your theatre key?"

"Why?" He was immediately suspicious.

"Oh," I said as casually as possible. "I've just realised I left my jacket and some other stuff in the theatre and I'll need it for school tomorrow. If you let me borrow the key, I can pop back and get it."

I don't think Grant was fooled for a minute, and I could tell by the look on her face that Mum wasn't taken in at all, but I think Grant was so weirded out by everything he had done in the past couple of hours – telling lies to the police, stashing a wanted man in his office – that Severn spreading his wings wouldn't have phased him. He just shrugged his acceptance, fished in his pocket and handed over the key.

"You'll need this as well," he said, returning to his desk and hurriedly writing a sequence of numbers on a memo pad and handing it to me. "That's the security code to get you back in here. Top one's the gate, bottom one's the door to the stairs."

"Thanks," I said, and I actually meant it.

"That was easy," Severn commented as we heard the lift doors close. "How long have we got?"

I looked at my watch.

"About three and a half hours." I grabbed one of the last few chips and threw out a question. "Do you still have to get on this plane?"

Severn fielded his one-eyebrow-raised questioning look. I continued.

"Originally you ran away because Seth is obviously some kind of psychopath and you thought he was going to kill you. Right? And then we hid you because by then we knew the cops wanted you for killing Tasha. Right? But you've already decided that you can handle Seth. And after tonight we'll be able to give the cops proof you didn't kill Tasha. So give me three good reasons why you still need to get on that plane."

I had hoped that the question would throw him and he wouldn't be able to come up with an answer. Instead, he stood up and began to pace around the small office, ticking the reasons off on his fingers.

"Reason one. Fingerprints. Mine. On their records and on the sound board. Plus that damned body the girls left at New Brighton that's just too close to the other one in Dunedin. That's just going to get too messy and I don't want to have to go there.

"Reason two. Seth may not scare me any more but he is still, as you said, a dangerous psychopath and right now, a very pissed off one. I am not so stupid that I don't want to keep some distance between us for a while.

"And reason three. The main reason. I am very, very, very angry about this whole deal. I want to see this monastery place. I want to find out what it's all about. And I want to get there before the others. Before the Reverend Father David Rochester. He's got these great plans to go back and haul Seth up on whatever charges he's concocting. And he's going to be the big guy. Not if I can help it. If I get there first, it'll be my side of the story they'll be getting, not his, and he will not come out looking good. What about that rubbish he was spouting to Finn about Meredith getting counselling? Come on! She's twice as evil as Olivia and he knows it. She kills people for kicks! That's just a blatant lie of David's to get them on his side for now because he's physically more scared of Seth than I am. He'll change his tune as soon as he doesn't need their support. No, I'm looking forward to getting on that plane. This could be fun!"

"Which is more than I can say for tonight. I'm getting nervous. Let's go and set up the theatre."

CHAPTER THIRTY ONE

After all the running and hiding, it seemed a bit surreal to walk casually down the street. Not that we were really being casual, just trying to look that way. Severn was in full hunting mode, tuned to every sound, choosing the best route with the fewest observers. I was so nervous. At every corner I expected to see a cop car. I think I held my breath all the way to the theatre. I felt relieved when we got there safely, but it was short-lived and quickly transmuted itself into a different kind of nervous. The game was on.

"I'll power up the lights and sound," Severn instructed. "You take the curtain up."

He bounded off to the equipment panel by the stage manager's station and started pushing buttons while I hauled on the rope that lifted the huge velvet curtains, opening the stage to the body of the theatre.

Watching Severn, he could have been preparing for any normal show, running through all the usual pre-show checks. Position himself behind the lighting board at the back of the audience, he pushed slider after slider, making the different lights glow and fade alternately. Finally a pool of amber lighting created a focal point on the centre of the stage.

"That'll do it," he said cheerfully, fading the lights and turning his attention to the soundboard.

"Sound check, please," he called to me and I obediently moved around the various microphones, talking into each one in turn and hearing my voice return to me over the speakers.

"Check one two," I repeated over and over till Severn was satisfied.

"Check one two, check one two," his voice came over the speakers as he ran identical checks on two of the portable radio mics.

"Here," he held one up to me, "clip this on."

I took it, clipping the tiny pack to my jeans, feeding the wire under my sweatshirt and clipping the microphone to the neckband.

"A slight change of plan," Severn suggested. "About the camera. I know you were thinking of using that one," he indicated vaguely in the direction of the Gods – the top tier of audience seats, "but it's a very wide-angle shot. I don't know if you are aware that there are two other cameras." I shook my head. "On the central lighting bar. One's focussed for close-ups on the back row of the chorus and the other is for side shots in the office scene. If I re-position those..."

He didn't need to finish the sentence, I was already nodding in agreement.

"I'll have to go up to the flys to drop in the lighting bar," he added, moving towards the ladder and beginning to climb.

After a couple of rungs, he reversed directions back to the stage floor and began to unbutton his shirt.

"It's a bit narrow across the shoulders for climbing ladders in," he explained as he draped it over a piece of set. "I can't afford to turn up at the airport with a ripped shirt."

'Fair enough." I wasn't complaining.

He climbed the ladder quickly and deftly lowered the lighting bar. Which just proves that vampires are stronger than they look because I know it usually took two men to haul one of those fully laden. Lights are heavy. Then he climbed back down and together we swung the cameras so they would both focus on the centre stage. Severn climbed back up the ladder to haul the massive bar back into place in the grid and I completed by scene setting by unlocking the stage door and wedging it slightly open. Maybe I'll take up directing. My show was starting to take shape. All I needed now was the star.

CHAPTER THIRTY TWO

The star came early. I had expected it. I would have done the same. I mean, if someone sends you a threatening letter telling you to be somewhere at a certain time, the most sensible thing you can do is arrive early, hopefully before they do. So, although my note said midnight, I was always working towards an eleven-thirty kick-off. Even so, I was grateful for Severn's vampire ears, as from my chosen vantage point in the flys, I didn't know anyone had arrived until Severn flicked on the lights to reveal my murderer, elegantly posed centre stage in a wash of flattering amber.

"Glad you could make it," Severn's voice, soft and menacing through the speakers, floated from everywhere and from nowhere.

"Where are you?" the figure on the stage looked around desperately, unable to penetrate the dazzle of the stage lights.

"Here." Severn's voice came from the left side of the stage. "And here," Now from the right. He was panning the sound from one speaker to another.

"And here," I added, knowing that he would have my radio mic channel up as well.

"What do you want?" Panic was setting in.

"The truth," I said, my voice eerily emanating from opposite to where I was hiding. "Why did you send Tasha that note? Why did you want to meet her here?"

"I didn't. What note?" My victim looked genuinely confused. My theory was right.

"The one Tasha had stuffed down her bra. 'Backstage, midnight', remember that? It was your handwriting. I recognised it. Tell you what, I'll tell you what I think happened and you can correct me when I go wrong. Okay?"

Severn was doing amazing things with my voice through the special effects unit. It was impossible to tell if I was male or female, or even human, and he was panning the speakers quickly, moving the sound around. Down on the stage my poor victim seemed to deflate in defeat. Sounding like some spooky theatre ghost, I continued.

"That note had nothing to do with Tasha did it? You gave it to Jason Broderick. You were meeting him here at midnight. Tasha found the note and she recognised your writing, just as I did.

Didn't she?"

"All right! Yes!" Dilys Davenport threw up her hands in surrender. "The little bitch found it in his pocket. She was always putting her hands in men's pockets." I thought back to the incident with the screwdriver. Dilly was telling the truth. She continued.

"She must have found it. She got here first. She was up in the fly tower with a camera. We were ... ah... here for a while ... before we realised she was there. Jason saw the flash. She laughed at me. Said the negatives would be worth an A pass on her exams. Talked about putting them on a website, or posting them to the school board of governors.

"Jason tried to coax her down. He suggested a threesome. She took her knickers off, threw them down to us, and suggested we come up to her. She was goading us. Let's do it in the fly tower. I pretended I thought it was a great idea and climbed up.

"She'd put the camera down to take her knickers off, so I grabbed at it. But she did too and we ended up both pulling at it. I had the camera and she had the strap. Then she tugged extra hard and the strap broke. She staggered backwards and fell over the railing. It was an accident. I didn't mean to kill her. It was an accident." Dilly broke down in tears.

I was about to tell Severn we had all we needed and we could wrap it up when, as Dilly always did, she rallied and came back on the attack.

"What do you want," she looked up, still trying to pinpoint my position. "Your note said you expected payment for silence. What's your price?"

That was when I made my big mistake. I moved fractionally and the board under my foot creaked. Dilly heard it and immediately knew where I was. Before I had realised my mistake, she was running across the stage and climbing the ladder. I was trapped in the flys. If I could get to the top of the ladder before she did, maybe I kick her hands off the rungs. I was thinking too slowly. She was moving too fast. Before I had got half way back along the walkway, she was up the ladder and facing me. As soon as I saw the expression on her face, I knew the rest of the story. It was reality tv, Crime Watch. We were going to re-enact the mysterious killing of the showgirl, with Riley Lowe starring as Natasha Moreland.

"Great acting down there, Miss Davenport." I was stalling

for time, hoping Severn would get here quickly. "The story was quite believable and those tears were very authentic. It's not what happened though, is it?"

That's the great thing about actors, they can't resist taking centre stage. Feed them the right cue and they're off, on autopilot. Dilly was no exception. She wanted to talk, to brag, to be the star.

"Not completely, no. There never was a camera. But the little bitch did get here before me. When she found the letter in Jason's pocket she confronted him and he lied. He told her that he had written it and was going to give it to her. He told her about the fire exit. Then he told me that he couldn't make it by midnight and could we meet later, nearer to one o'clock. The bastard was going to meet her first. But I got here at twelve. When I arrived she and Jason were already hard at it. Up here in the fly tower. They were so busy they didn't even hear me arrive. It was too simple. I just climbed up, hauled her off and shoved her."

"And Jason let you?"

"Huh!" Dilly snorted her disgust. "There wasn't much he could do with his pants around his ankles."

'Why didn't he tell the police? Why is he acting like he doesn't know anything?"

"Because, my dear Riley, he has just as much to lose as I do. If I go down, I take him with me."

"He didn't do anything." I wasn't following this.

"Tasha Moreland was under age. Her mother used to home school her. When she came to high school she was away ahead of her age group. In spite of those boobs and that attitude, she was only fourteen."

"You're joking!" I was genuinely shocked.

"How would that have looked on Jason's file?" Dilly snorted. "He's about to cut a million dollar movie deal. The last thing he can afford right now is a sex scandal. Trust me, Jason has every reason to shut up. You, on the other hand, strike me as just the sort of silly bitch who would rush off to the police and there is no way I am going to let that happen. It looks as if silly little Riley, school friend of the deceased, broke into the theatre late at night and was climbing around the fly tower in the dark when she had a dreadful accident − just like her friend Natasha. Or" Dilly paused for effect, "the police might just be forced to expand their search for her boyfriend who is obviously a serial killer."

"Maybe I am." Severn approached stealthily from behind

her. "But maybe she's not my next victim."

Dilly spun around as she realised that she was trapped now, not me. She rushed at him, trying to push past him to reach the ladder. He grabbed her arm but she fought back like a cat, scratching at him with her long red nails and kicking randomly, hoping to connect. Severn kept his grip. She changed tactics, suddenly slumping down as if exhausted, then just as quickly, punching a tightly balled fist into his crotch. Severn collapsed instantly and Dilly shook herself free to turn on me. Launching herself from a crouching start like a sprinter in a running race, she sprang forwards. I stood my ground till the last second than stepped aside. Powered by her own momentum, Dilys Davenport sailed over the edge of the fly tower to the stage floor below.

CHAPTER THIRTY THREE

Severn pulled himself to his feet, wincing with pain, and joined me at the edge.

"She fell off," I said obviously. He laughed.

"No shit! And I only got the first confession, the fake one, on tape. I stopped the cameras just before she rushed at you and I just got here as fast as I could, I didn't think about turning the cameras back on. Sorry."

"No, that's fine. It doesn't really matter much. Maybe it makes it easier. At least for Jason."

"You give a toss about Jason?"

"No, not really. But living with it has to be punishment enough, doesn't it?"

"Depends how long you live," Severn replied enigmatically.

"Messy, messy!" A voice penetrated from the blackness offstage.

Looking like rejects from the Matrix, Seth, Olivia and Meredith sauntered onto the stage and looked down at the crumpled heap that used to be Dilys Davenport. Even from the flys I could see the spreading pool of blood. Meredith knelt down, dipped her finger in it and tasted it like it was chocolate.

"Go ahead girls," Seth invited. "Shame to waste it."

"Don't be so disgusting," I called out.

"Oh, tsk, tsk," Seth relied sardonically. "Don't be so squeamish. It's not like she needs it any more. Care to join us Severn? You must be starving by now."

I glanced at Severn and could tell by the quick way his tongue flicked over his lips that Seth was right. I had to keep reminding myself that Severn was still a vampire. It was easy to see Seth and the girls as B-grade movie nasties, especially in the black leathers they were currently sporting, but it was a lot harder to remember that Severn was one of them too. He looked so much ... well... nicer! But he was still a vampire – and one who hadn't fed for nearly a week.

"She'd be much more fun. Can we have her instead?" Meredith inquired in her pretty little girly voice, pointing up at me. "Are you going to share your snack with us voluntarily, Sev darling, or do we have to come up and get her?"

"No!" I clung to Severn, genuinely scared.

"And just how do you expect your little superhero to save you then?" Seth laughed.

"He could gather her into his arms and fly off into the sunset," Meredith chanted. "Oops! No he can't. You haven't learnt to fly yet, have you sweetie?"

"Pathetic, isn't it?" Seth inquired. "Over a hundred years and he still can't flap his wings. But he doesn't need us to remind him how inadequate he is. He knows that. He also knows perfectly well that right at this very moment, we hold a full set of cards and he holds absolutely none at all. There are only two ways down out of that fly tower – the ladder, or the more direct route favoured by the late Miss Davenport here. Which way would you prefer to travel, Miss Lowe?"

With a growing sense of impending doom, I realised he was right. We were trapped. Either we climbed down the ladder or they would come up and get us. There had to be another way. Looking desperately for an alternate way out, I spotted something useful. High in the grid above us I could see a wooden pole, one of the type used to anchor the bottom of the backcloths, left behind by the riggers. If only we could reach it.

It was one of those rare flashes of mental clarity when the whole universe suddenly makes sense. Or at least your small part of it. All through the year at school they had been constantly reminding us that it was our final year. Come December we faced the big world of grown-ups. It was time to think about the future. Time to start making decisions about a future career. I had been studiously trying to avoid thinking about it. All of a sudden it was obvious. If I wanted a future that was longer than the next ten minutes.

Acting more scared than I felt, I snuggled closer into Severn, pressing my face into his chest. He fell into my plan and hugged me tight. He had forgotten about the scratches inflicted in his struggle with Dilly, still oozing blood. I put my mouth against one and sucked hard.

Severn gasped and jumped back but it was too late. I felt the warm taste of blood in my mouth. A taste I was going to have to get used to. We both realised the enormity of what I had done. I wondered perversely how long it took to grow wings and whether Mum would notice.

"Now take him out," I whispered.

"Oh yes, please do," Seth replied. "Yes, I heard that, Miss

Lowe. And I am all aquiver waiting to see how he's going to do it."
He might have heard what I said, but with the stage lights blinding
them, they hadn't seen what I had just done. Advantage to us.
Play on.

Knowing they couldn't see me, but taking no chances, I
turned my back to the stage and, using tiny movements masked
by my body, gestured frantically. I pointed to the pole, pointed to
Severn, made little flapping motions with my hands, pointed to
Seth then pretended to stab myself in the chest. Severn got the
message and nodded almost imperceptibly. He gestured back,
pointing to me, to Seth and moving his hands like ducks quacking.
I had to keep Seth talking, provide a distraction. I gave him the
thumbs up.

While Severn stepped as far back into the shadows as
possible and began to flex and unfurl his wings, I moved forwards,
closer towards the ladder and the front of the stage, picking up
the beltpack of the flyman's comms as I passed.

"So Seth," I called out cheerily, "If I do come down
voluntarily, what are you offering? I'm good backstage and I know
your secret. Can I join you? I'm sure Olivia and Meredith could
teach me all sorts of fun things."

I glanced back at Severn who gave me a nod, and I hurled
the comms as hard as I could at the nearest stage light. As I
expected, it exploded spectacularly, raining glass on those below.
All three vampires spun around in surprise. It was enough. Severn
jumped. I held my breath as he fell between the backcloths, his
wings folded upwards. What if they wouldn't work? Then they
spread wide and flapped twice and he soared upwards into the
grid.

By this time Seth had realised what was happening. He
started tearing at his long leather coat, trying hurriedly to strip
down and take to the air. It was too late. With deadly accuracy
Severn speared the pole into Seth's chest, the force of the throw
pinning Seth to the stage floor. Meredith screamed.

I climbed down the ladder, giggling slightly as I watched
Severn make a rather ungainly touchdown. I guess landing takes
practice. While he advanced menacingly towards the two girls,
who were rapidly backing up into a corner, I checked out the two
bodies. Dilly was most definitely dead, her eyes staring blankly,
her body twisted into a shape even a dancer would never achieve
while alive. So much blood from one person. Seth was still

twitching. I didn't go too close. Still keeping an eye on the girls, Severn picked up Seth's coat and rummaged in the pocket, pulling out a cell phone. He flicked through the numbers and speed dialled.

"David. Severn. Get your butt down to the theatre now! We have some cleaning up to do."

"Don't move!" he ordered Olivia and Meredith. Then with a flick of his wings, he flew upwards into the grid, returning with the two videos he had removed from the cameras, which he handed to me.

"Go," he said. "We'll leave Dilys here. Edit those films and get them to the police anonymously. They'll think she confessed and committed suicide. That'll get me off the hook and keep good old Jason in the clear."

"What about Seth?"

Severn gave a cold, nasty laugh.

"I guess the plane will have some excess baggage. David and the girls can package him up neatly for travel, can't you girls?"

They nodded in mute agreement.

"What about me?" I had to ask.

'Yeah!" Severn took my hands in his. "What about you?" he asked quietly. "You have no idea what you've let yourself in for. I wish now that I could take you with me, but right now that isn't possible. Too much has to be settled first. I promise I will email you as soon as I'm safe. We'll take it from there. In the meantime, go! Get back to the office, phone Grant and get him to pick you up. Don't mention any of this, just tell him David has taken me to the airport early. Stick to a simple story. You came to the theatre about nine o'clock, collected your jacket and left. There was no dead Dilys when you came, and none when you left. Okay?"

"No," I disagreed. "I never came here at all. I changed my mind, it was too cold."

I put my hands to my neck, fumbling for the gold chain that hung there. Shaking, I unclipped the tiny bluebird and, pulling Severn's head down so I could reach, fastened it around his neck. Now both birds could fly.

We hugged and kissed one last time. Then I turned and ran, clutching the precious videos. I didn't stop until I reached Grant's office block and was safely behind the carpark gates. Panting hard, I punched in the security code to open the door and sank down onto the stairs. I had better get my breath back before phoning home.

In the quiet glow of the security lamp, I looked down and realised my hands were covered with Dilly's blood. I should find the toilets and clean up. Still puffing, I climbed the stairs to the washroom and pushed my hands into the hot, gushing water.

The water ran red and Severn was gone.

Other Books by J.L. O'Rourke

Chains of Blood

The Second of Severn.

Riley Lowe is backstage at another show, but this time she is out of her depth, running equipment she doesn't understand and faced with all sorts of problems including a boy actor who is a spoilt little brat. When her personal vampires arrive to help, Riley thinks everything has suddenly got better, until the boy disappears. Will the vampire's special skills be enough to find the boy and how long will it be before Riley turns into a vampire herself?

Read an excerpt:

I fished a hanky out of my pocket, dried my eyes and blew my nose. Crying was not going to help. But I still had no idea what to do. Maybe Mum and Grant could help. The sound operator from our own theatre company was out of town touring with a fashion show but if Grant could get hold of him, he could at least tell me what to do.

Then my cell phone vibrated in my pocket. I hauled it out and stared at it blankly. A message from a withheld number. Curious, I opened it.

"angels r us look up look left"

I looked up, peered through the darkness of the encroaching night. Looked left – towards the carpark. And they were there. Three figures emerged out of the gloom, striding side by side like the baddies in a b-grade western or the chorus-line for a musical version of the Matrix, long black coats flowing behind them. Before I could get out of my chair the one in the middle had broken into a run. I have never climbed down the scaffold as quickly, but I was still not at ground level when he reached me, picked me off the scaffold and pulled me into his arms.

When I came up for breath I could see Mum and Grant standing up from where they had been sitting on the grass and walking towards David and Aiden, hands outstretched in welcome.

"What? How? When?" I stuttered, wrapping my arms around Severn's waist under his coat as we walked to join the others.

"Sounded like you needed help," Severn smiled, his arm around my shoulders.

"And we needed sun," Aiden added.

I gave him a quizzical look. "You? Needed sun? Umm...?" The "have you forgotten you're a vampire?" question left unasked.

"Oh no, not in the want-to-hang-out-in-the-daylight way. We were just sick of snow. It is so cold in the mountains."

"And we were bored," the Reverend added. "Sounds like we got here just at the right time. We were in the carpark. We heard the director's little request."

Of course they did. A normal person sitting beside me wouldn't have heard it unless they were wearing headphones but of course the vampires heard it. I wonder how long it takes for things like that to change – my hearing hadn't changed at all yet and it had been three months since I had drunk Severn's blood and started the change-over. I must ask them how long it takes and what the symptoms are.

"How did you get here so quickly? I only emailed you yesterday?"

"We flew," Severn replied with one of his pedantically correct and obvious answers, complete with raised eyebrow over his fine, tortoiseshell-rimmed glasses.

I gave him a similar look back. "Flew? Um, flew... as in...?"

"As in the Lear Jet," Severn laughed. "You weren't thinking...?" and he flexed his shoulders so I could feel his wings move under his t-shirt. "We are not that fast – or that fit."

"Weren't you worried about coming back so soon after ... what if they stopped you at the airport? Don't the police still want to talk to you about the body at New Brighton?"

Severn smiled and pulled a passport out of his coat pocket. I looked at the name – Benedict Bailey. The passport was French.

"Benedict Bailey?" I whispered. "Is your passport guy an alcoholic or something? You left here as Father John Benedictine on a Vatican passport, now you're named after two types of drink, not just one." I shook my head in disbelief. Severn laughed.

"So who are you in public? Severn or Benny?"

"You could just yell, hey you. That could work."

"Riley!" Danny came up behind us. "I've spoken to the stage

manager, to the president and to the director but got no-where. We have to find all this extra gear tomorrow and make it work. Sorry. I am going to be struggling just to get my lighting stuff. I will ask around to see if anyone can help with the sound stuff, but I can't promise anything."

"Sorted." The Reverend stepped forward. "I'm David Rochester. We've worked with Grant's company before and we heard yesterday that Riley was struggling, so we've come to help."

Danny tilted his head to the side quizzically and looked down at the diminutive figure in the enveloping ankle-length coat. I could tell what he was thinking. The Rev was even shorter than me with long hair pulled back in a pony tail. He looked like a doll. Danny gave Severn and Aiden an equally hard appraisal that seemed to last for ages before breaking into a wide smile. He grabbed the Rev's hand and shook it firmly. "Welcome aboard. Any of you do lighting?"

"We all do," the Rev replied. "We're a professional crew, we all do everything."

"Oh halleluiah! That is the best thing I have heard all week! Let's talk later. In the meantime, Riley, they want us at our desks. Act 2."

Severn joined me at the sound desk and I was happy to let him tweak the dials as his super-sensitive ears picked up all the faults in the mix. He couldn't fix the faults in the acting. As the hour got later, the actors got more and more tired and made more and more mistakes until half way through the act the director called it quits. Which was fine for the actors, but Danny and I still had about an hour's work packing up all the gear and stowing it back in the container. Well, an hour's work without three strong vampires. With them the pack-out was just finishing as Mum and Grant arrived in the carpark.

"Where are you staying?" Mum asked.

"We've booked a motel a couple of blocks from your place," the Rev replied.

"Can I go with them?" I asked.

Mum smiled. "Of course. Just... um... oh," her hands flapped as she struggled. "Just for coffee. Don't stay out too late."

I knew what she wasn't saying but was thinking

The motel lady's suspicious look said that she was obviously thinking the same thing. I guess we did look a bit strange. All in black, none of us looking older than teenagers and arriving close to midnight. Still, she handed over the key to the unit and pointed out where we could park the guys' rental car. Inside, the unit was really nice – two bedrooms, a bathroom and a lounge with a tiny but complete kitchen. Severn grabbed the room with the queen-size bed; the Rev and Aiden making rude comments as they threw their bags on the two single beds in the other room. Then over cups of coffee I filled them in on my disasters and they outlined their plans to fix them. Tomorrow they would all source and pack in the extra gear, including helping Danny to rig his tower, then Severn would take over the sound desk, Aiden and I would do radio mics and the Rev would trouble-shoot all other disasters. I stopped panicking. From now on the show was going to be fun.

I had lots of questions for them too, but Aiden suggested that Severn should take me home. It was nearly two o'clock in the morning and I was exhausted, so even though I really wanted to stay with Severn, I knew Aiden was right. Severn drove me home and pulled into the driveway. As I unclipped my seatbelt, he pulled me close. His kiss was rough, hungry, almost brutal. I wanted to pull away but I wanted it never to stop. I kissed him back just as hard. Our hands moved over each other, finding their way under the layers of clothing. I slipped my hands around his back, feeling his wings tremble as I ran my finders down their furled ridge. He moaned, pulling me tighter. I knew he wanted to turn the car around and drive back to the motel, to the queen-sized bed, and part of me wanted him to do just that. Then a light came on in the house and I knew Mum and Grant were waiting up for me. I also knew that when I got inside they would pretend that they weren't, that it was just coincidence that they happened to wake up when I arrived, but that wouldn't be true. The knowledge that they were hovering, probably peeking out through the curtains, spoiled the moment and, suddenly, instead of enjoying the kiss, I felt like the whole world was watching. I pulled away.

"I think I had better go," I explained, pulling a sad face.

"Yes, I guess so." Severn sounded annoyed. "I think you are expected."

So, with mixed feelings of elation and frustration, I let myself out of the car and ran up the drive to the front door, which opened magically as I approached.

"Oh, hello," Mum failed to sound genuinely surprised. "I thought I heard something – must have been the car. I guess I don't have to ask you if you've had a good evening. See you in the morning. Good night."

As she walked off down the passage towards her bedroom, I could hear her softly singing something that sounded suspiciously like the theme from "Lost Boys", her favourite vampire movie. Sometimes Mum is just plain creepy!

Power Ride

An Avi Livingstone Murder Mystery

Kester (Kit) Simmons, drummer with the rock band 'Charlotte Jane', was out of beat. He was stressed out, starving and he thought he was going crazy. Then, with less than two weeks to go before a national tour, Kit's precious drums and one of the band members are found slashed to pieces. The keyboard player, Avi Livingstone, is missing, Kit has no alibi and, to make matters worse, the police suspect him of dealing drugs.

Read an excerpt:

The weary-looking blond was not amused.

"Stop!" His shouted command cut through the sound pumping from the Marshall amplifiers, stopping his five fellow musicians in mid bar.

"Hold it!" The blond spun round to face the drummer.

"Kit, it's no bloody good, man. It's not bloody working. And it's not bloody good enough. What's with you, man? This is old hat! We've done it a million times, a dozen already today. You're always telling me you can do this number in your sleep; so sleep then, because today you sure as hell can't do it when you're awake!"

The man half-hidden behind the rack of shining black Tama drums moved both his sticks to his right hand, freeing his left to push a lock of long, sweat-dampened black hair back into place.

"I'm sorry," he said softly. "It's just... I'm a bit... um... I'm just not very together."

"We noticed."

"Look, can we take a break? I don't feel so good."

The blond shrugged and, as an answer, unstrapped his ageing Gibson guitar and propped it up onto a conveniently placed support stand.

"Why not? It certainly can't make this damned rehearsal go any worse."

Kester Simmons pushed the unruly lock of hair back into place again then unthreaded his long, lean body from behind his drums.

"I really am sorry, Danny," he sighed.

The blond replied with a savage glare.

"I don't want apologies, Kit, I want a drum beat. Damn it all, Kit, it just isn't good enough. We are hitting the road on tour in just over a week - ten days to be precise - and this rehearsal has been a complete bloody disaster!" Daniel Gordon was working himself into a mild frenzy.

Kester turned to walk away but Danny had wound himself up and continued his harangue.

"And another thing, Mr Simmons! If your 'not feeling too good' means what it usually does, you'd better get your act together and you had better do it damned fast. It's a long tour and we're not babysitting you through it this time. You had better be on deck all the bloody way!" His voice dropped to a malicious hiss. "Don't you forget for one minute, Kit, that we are running real close to not making this tour at all, and it's all your fault."

"Hey, come on now!"

"That's below the belt!" The keyboard player and the rhythm guitarist leapt simultaneously to Kit's defence.

"That was below the belt and decidedly uncalled for," the rhythm guitarist, Mike Kiesanowski, repeated himself. "We are slightly behind schedule because our bass player quit. That was not Kit's fault and we are getting mighty sick of you hassling him about it."

"Huh!" Danny snorted in fury and stormed off towards the coffee-making facilities at the other end of the old converted carpenter's workshop the band used as a permanent rehearsal venue.

Without acknowledging Mike's spirited defence of him, Kit dropped his drumsticks into his gear bag and headed out the door into the garden which formed the surroundings for both the rehearsal room and Kit's own quaint little settler's cottage. Once outside he leaned his back against the wall, took a couple of deep breaths, ran both hands through his hair in a sign of despair then began a methodical but unsuccessful search of his pockets for a packet of cigarettes. Finding none, he muttered an unintelligible curse and slid down the wall into a sitting position. A few seconds later another figure flung itself down beside him and placed an arm around Kit's shoulders.

"You okay?"

Kit looked at the concerned expression behind the gold-rimmed glasses that framed the keyboard player's face and gave a wan smile.

"I'm not great, but I'll live." His smile opened into the hopeful, innocent expression normally seen on spaniel pups. "Hey, you wouldn't have a spare cigarette by any chance?"

Avi Livingstone pulled a squashed packet of Rothmans from the hip pocket of his ancient, faded Levis. He flicked it open but it revealed only the tattered remains of a cigarette which Avi threw away.

"Sorry, Kit, that's it. How come you're scavenging again anyway? Can't you afford your own?"

"Um... no," Kit replied apologetically. "I'm broke."

Avi sat back and his soulful brown eyes subjected Kit to a long, searching appraisal.

"Look, Kit," he said eventually, "I know it's none of my business but was Danny's comment on the mark? I mean, you're broke already, and it's still early in the week, you say you're not feeling very well and, let's face it, your drumming's been half a beat off all morning."

Avi let the comment hang in the air but Kit declined to answer, content to scuff the ground in front of him with the toe of his boot. Avi patted Kit gently on the shoulder.

"Come on, Kit, this is Avi. An honest answer, okay?"

Kit rounded on him, flicked Avi's hand away and snapped a reply.

"An honest answer? Oh yeah? And you're all going to believe me, just like that? I know what you all think. It doesn't matter what I say, you'll all believe whatever you damned well want to. And I suppose you'll be checking up on me with Gabriel behind my back."

"Hey, come on, calm down." Avi gently restrained Kit from getting up and leaving. "Calm down. I repeat, this is Avi you're talking to, not Danny, not Gabriel. I believe you. I always believe you. When have I ever not believed you? Come on, now, talk to me, what's wrong?"

"Sorry." Kit slumped back against the wall. "Honest answer? I'm broke because my money's been cut back again and I can't manage, not that I ever could. Mum and Gabriel said I got behind on the power and phone bills, even though I was sure that I'd been keeping up, so they've taken power of attorney over my money again. Gabriel pays everything for me and gives me a pathetically small amount of pocket money, which leads me back to my original statement - I'm broke!"

"Power of attorney? Can they do that at your age?"

"Oh yeah, you'd better believe they can! All my money is handled by them through a trust anyway, since I was in hospital last time, so I can't do anything about it - except grovel desperately."

"And you've been a naughty boy and spent your allowance already," Avi teased.

"Don't rub it in, it's humiliating enough."

"Sorry"

"Yeah, so I've got no cigarettes and Mum's out of town today so I couldn't phone her and hit her up for a loan - not that she'd give me money for cigarettes anyway. I'd just get yet another moralising lecture on the virtues of quitting. In answer to your other accusations, I know I'm drumming like an epileptic praying mantis but I'm not feeling very well and I don't feel well because I'm pretty stressed out. But it's just that, Avi, stress. I am not - repeat not - underlined, in capital letters not - stoned. Okay? Get that? Not stoned! Out of all of them, Avi, you should know I've been clean for over a year. You guys are as bad as Mum and Gabriel. They don't trust me either."

"Of course I trust you. I was just worried. Hey, if you're stressed out it's because something's bothering you. Can I help in any way? I'm here any time you need me, you know that. Do you want to talk about it?"

"Thanks, but no thanks. I'll be okay. I just need a cigarette."

Eighteen years of friendship had taught Avi when not to push Kit, so he backed off, lightening the tone.

"Tell you what then, why don't we leave Danny to cool off and sneak down to the dairy. I'll buy us a packet of cigarettes and we can share them."

"Um... I don't know when I can pay you back."

"So, who's counting? Leave it to me in your will," Avi grinned as he hauled Kit's lanky body to its feet. "Come on, before the pocket battleship launches another offensive."

By the time the two men had returned to the workshop Daniel Gordon had left. The band's replacement bass player, Kelly Reynolds, their temporary backing vocalist, Joanna Greenwood, and Mike Kiesanowski were ensconced comfortably in three of the dilapidated arm chairs which formed a casual semi-circle around the primitive coffee-making facilities at the far end of the large room. Avi and Kit slumped into two of the other chairs, Kit completing the act by stretching his long legs out to rest silver decorated, black leather boots on the badly stained coffee table. Joanna lifted her tiny trainer-clad foot and kicked Kit's off the table.

"Get your feet off the table, you lanky slob!"

"It's my table," Kit argued petulantly, although he obliged, but only because Joanna had pushed his feet off and he couldn't find the energy to put them back on.

"So where's our beloved leader?" asked Avi, craning his neck to scan the room.

"He gave up on you lot, called you by all sorts of interesting descriptive phrases - especially you, Kit, then ordered a lunch break," Mike replied. "We have two hours of carefree liberty after which he expects us to perform - or else!"

"That wasn't how he phrased it," Joanna smiled.

"No, that's the edited version fit for human consumption."

"Great," said Avi. "So why are you lot still hanging around here?"

"We were awaiting your return to ascertain whether or not you wished to accompany us to luncheon."

Avi grinned at the young man who had given the pompous-sounding reply. Kelly Reynolds was a recent arrival to the group and was still somewhat of an enigma. Mike, Avi and Kit were founding members of the group, 'Charlotte Jane', and were old friends from way back. Mike had met Avi and Kit when the band was first formed; Avi and Kit went back even further, to their first days at Beckenham Primary School eighteen years before. Joanna, although new to the group, was a long-standing acquaintance. She was Avi's cousin and in the tight-knit world of their parent's religious community the two had grown up closely together. Danny Gordon wasn't a local by birth, but he had been around long enough to be considered part of the Christchurch musical establishment. He came originally from Geraldine, a small rural community south of Christchurch, but generally chose not to broadcast that fact too widely. Daniel Gordon had a serious self-image problem.

Kelly Reynolds, on the other hand, seemed eminently self-assured. He had a different style to the others. His short, trendy haircut and snappy fashion clothing contrasted markedly with the more traditional 'long-haired scruffy rock musician' image of Kit and Avi, and his way of speaking matched his style. It wasn't as if he was being consciously pompous either. Kelly came from an upper-crust Wellington family and had all the benefits of an expensive private school education. The accent came naturally, along with an eclectic knowledge of world affairs, an innate sense of style and, as Joanna had often noted, an elegant, almost balletic, way of moving. To Joanna's eyes, at least, Kelly was a very tasty package.

Kelly acknowledged Avi's grin at his accent with a slight bow of his head. He grinned back and continued, "Then the telephone rang for Kester."

Kit looked up, flicking the hair out of his eyes with a gesture that was so habitual it had been become almost subconscious.

"Who was it?" he asked.

"I'm afraid I don't know," Kelly shrugged. "He didn't say. He merely inquired if Kester Simmons, and he did use Kester, not Kit, was there. I said you had disappeared temporarily with Avrahim and that we had placed bets on the probable destination being the corner dairy. Fair guess? Anyway, I inquired if I could take a message but he declined and hung up. I'm afraid he failed to leave a name or a contact number."

He shrugged his shoulders expressively and stared at Kit whose face now registered a broad grin.

"Yes!" Kit shouted, punching the air with a fist. "Awesome!"

Joanna turned to Avi. "That makes sense to you, does it?"

Avi grinned and shook his head.

"No, but that's normal with Kit, he never makes any sense."

"Well, I have no intentions of playing guessing games, especially when I haven't been fed. To hell with you guys, I'm going to find some lunch. There is no way I am going to put up with any more of Daniel Gordon's little hissy fits on an empty stomach." So saying, Jo pulled an orange nylon parka from the back of the chair in which Kelly was languidly sprawled, thrust her arms into the jacket's sleeves and headed purposely towards the door.

"You know something?" Kelly said to no-one in particular, "The lovely lady has made an infinitely practical suggestion. Shall we join her?"

There was a general mumbling of agreement as the men rose to their feet and trooped out to follow Jo. As the party wended its way around Oxford Terrace, Joanna dropped back to fall into step with Avi.

"Cousin, tell me something. Kit's a bit out of it, isn't he? Do tours always have this effect on him?"

"Tours? No, they don't affect him at all, strangely enough," Avi replied thoughtfully. "Something is obviously bugging him, though. Mind you, that doesn't mean to say that it'll be anything horrendous. Kit doesn't have the most stable personality and he is apt to make monstrous mountains out of the most minute of molehills. Whatever it is, he doesn't want to talk about it. This, with Kit, means that it is probably something reasonably serious, but I can't force him to talk to me. I'll have another go later. I can usually convince him to talk, it's just a matter of easing him along gently. I can be very persuasive." He ignored Jo's expression of sarcasm. "I wouldn't worry about it too much, though. In the meantime, I would think the best thing we can do is keep Danny from ripping Kit's face off this afternoon."

"Danny doesn't like Kit much, does he?"

"Huh!" Avi's laugh was more a scoff of derision. "Rest assured, cousin dearest, it's nothing personal. This close to a tour, Danny hates everyone, including and especially himself. Tours might not affect Kit, but they blow Danny away. He'll get worse yet."

"Super." Jo did not sound as if she actually meant the superlative. "You mean we're likely to see some fireworks?"

"Better than Old Man Carson's bonfires. I guarantee it."

Joanna laughed and rubbed her hands gleefully. Then she stopped and looked serious.

"But Danny's such a little guy. He wouldn't be stupid enough to upset the whole band would he? Surely?"

"He would, he has and he will, no doubt, do so again. In case you hadn't noticed, Daniel Gordon is somewhat akin to your neighbour's crazed Jack Russell terrier. Wind him up enough and he'll tackle anything, even if it is three times his size. Mind you, we could have some real problems this tour. I don't think it's going to be a very smooth ride. Danny is still very angry about losing our last bass player and, even though we've got Kelly, Danny is determined to hold Kit responsible and to rub it in as much as possible."

"Why?"

Avi shrugged his shoulders and spread his hands wide in a gesture of genuine incomprehension.

"I don't know. Danny's just a creep, I guess."

"So why keep him in the band, if he's such a creep?"

"Two reasons, I guess. He's a damn good guitarist and vocalist and he sells records."

"Garbage! The band sells records, not Danny Gordon. 'Charlotte Jane' was selling records before Danny joined you guys, and who the hell was he? Some two-bit wanna-be from Geraldine! Come on, Avi, he might be a good guitarist but they're ten a penny. If the man is a jerk you've got to have a better reason than that for keeping him on."

Avi ran his hand thoughtfully over his unshaven chin. He shrugged again.

"You know something, Jo? I don't have a decent answer. I guess we've got so used to Danny being a prize prick we just take his temper tantrums for granted. I mean, nobody's perfect, and if we started throwing out band members who had personality problems there'd be bugger all of us left. Poor old Kit would be at the top of the list, he's completely scrambled, and I don't think I'm always the easiest musician to work with. Anyway, whatever Danny is, he's a good businessman. He's got a pretty watertight contract, so we're stuck with him for the duration, at least."

"The duration of what?"

"The cd, the tour and the next single. It could be an exhausting few months."

About the Author

J. L. O'Rourke has worked as a journalist, sub-editor, free-lance writer and office administrator. When not writing, she enjoys being in a theatre, either onstage as a singer or backstage where she has been everything from floor crew to stage-manager. She lives in Christchurch, New Zealand, with an assortment of hairless dogs, fluffy cats and grumpy guinea pigs.

You can email her at
mailto:editor@millwheelpress.co.nz
or follow her on Facebook at
https://www.facebook.com/MillwheelPress
or on Smashwords,
https://www.smashwords.com/profile/view/millwheel